The Mystery of the Other Girl

Wylly Folk St. John
The Mystery of the Other Girl

Illustrated by Frank Aloise

AN AVON  CAMELOT BOOK

AVON BOOKS
A division of
The Hearst Corporation
959 Eighth Avenue
New York, New York 10019

First Camelot Printing, February, 1978

CAMELOT TRADEMARK REG. U.S. PAT. OFF. AND IN
OTHER COUNTRIES, MARCA REGISTRADA, HECHO EN
U.S.A.

Printed in the U.S.A.

This book, with love, is for Jenny and Chuck and their friends in Florida.

*About
the Author*

WYLLY FOLK ST. JOHN is a true Southerner. She was
born in South Carolina, spent her childhood in Savannah,
graduated from the University of Georgia in Athens, and
is now living in Social Circle, not far from Atlanta. She
was employed as a staff writer for the Magazine Section of
the *Atlanta Journal and Constitution* for many years.

Contents

🌸 Who Is Morna Ross?

Everything was quiet in the Barron family room that Saturday afternoon—until the phone rang.

The rain that was giving the Florida Gulf Coast its wettest August on record was falling so hard that even Lyle wouldn't go out in it, though it was time to give Sport, his pet walking catfish, his supervised exercise crossing the yard and back. Today it would have been a swim—the yard was no drier than Sport's tank in the bathroom.

Lyle was considering his unlikely chances of getting Mom to let Sport take a walk across the family room; at the same time he was perfecting a card trick he hoped would mystify his sister Stevie if she ever came out of her room. Mom was sewing patches on the knees of Lyle's green jeans. The dripping noise of the rain accompanied the little piping sound of Stevie's flute as she practiced "The Gallant Eagle March" in her room, sitting cross-legged on her bed (Lyle knew from peeking through the keyhole). She was doing the flute part over and over, her eyes fixed on the poster of Simon and

Garfunkel that adorned her ceiling. Stevie had made first flute in the Lanham High band last term when she was only a ninth grader. She even had the white band sweater with the green emblem on it. She had to keep in practice all summer if she wanted to wear that green-and-gold uniform again next year.

Then the shrill *r-r-rrr-rrr-rrring* shattered the calm.

Mrs. Barron was nearest the phone; she picked it up before Stevie could get there, though Stevie beat Lyle by a nose. "Hello?" Then their mother's tone changed; there was a note of apprehension in it. "Long distance? What? I can't hear distinctly—Mobile? Did you say Mobile? This is Mrs. Frank Barron."

By this time Stevie had her ear against the receiver too, close to her mother's. Daddy was out of town on business and though he often phoned just to make sure they were O.K., particularly during storms, Stevie had a moment of anxiety. But then she remembered he always dialed direct, not through the operator. This couldn't be Daddy.

While this was going through Stevie's head, she was trying to hear what was being said; the Gulf storm gave them a terrible connection. Eventually through the static she made out a girl's voice saying, "May I please speak to John Henderson?"

Stevie was surprised and showed it. "She means Ian!" she told her mother.

"It's for Super-Boy?" Lyle asked, puzzled. "Here?"

"Yes—Ian—" the girl's distant voice said.

"Oh." Mrs. Barron tried to hide a little smile. "I'm sorry," she said to the girl on the phone. "He doesn't actually live here, though you might think so—he's here often enough. But he's not here now."

"Mother!" Stevie said reproachfully, moving back from the phone a bit so the girl couldn't hear her. "Ian and I broke up—"

"Oh?" Her mother listened to the voice on the phone, a worried, pleading sort of voice. The girl was saying, "Could you tell me where I might reach him, please?"

Stevie muttered his home telephone number; she knew she would never forget it, no matter how many other boys she might date. Ian had been the very first boy she had ever loved. Right now she didn't see how she could have—but you can't help being sentimental about your first love. Mrs. Barron repeated the number into the phone.

"I've already tried that one," the girl said, "from Information. Mrs. Henderson referred me to your number."

"His mother doesn't know we broke up, I guess," Stevie said. "Let me—please, Mother."

Mrs. Barron shrugged and handed over the phone. Stevie said in her best grown-up manner, "May I ask who is calling, please?" She couldn't stand not knowing for another minute. She might give the girl Tiger's number, where Ian's rock band was probably rehearsing. And then, she might not.

She could hear the operator's clipped voice saying,

"Ma'am"—and Stevie almost giggled out loud—"may the party know who is calling?"

The girl's voice was clearer to Stevie now that she held the receiver to her own ear. It was a funny, soft, burry voice, kind of the way velvet would sound if it made a noise—not like anybody's voice Stevie knew. "Why, I guess so," she said. "This is Morna Ross. I—"

And then Stevie distinctly heard a scream.

It was as if the girl had been startled by somebody who frightened her. But the scream was stifled—as if somebody had suddenly put a hand over her open mouth. Then there was nothing but a dial tone. They had been cut off.

"What's the matter?" Lyle asked, interested. "You're looking at that phone like it was my walking catfish about to bite you—not that old Sport would bite you, if you'd just make friends with him. Hang it up, why don't you? I'm expecting an important call from Munro."

"That's all I need," Stevie said hysterically. "A walking catfish named Sport for a friend."

"What happened?" Mother asked.

"Mother, she screamed! She had just said, 'This is Morna Ross,' and then she screamed and somebody grabbed her and stopped up her mouth and hung up the phone. Mother, it's the strangest thing I ever heard of."

"It really is odd," Mother agreed. "Getting the call at all is strange enough. But maybe it wasn't a scream.

Maybe it was just some effect of the storm on the wires."

"No. It was a real scream," Stevie said positively. "About the realest scream I ever heard. Mother, who do you suppose Morna Ross could be?"

"What kind of a crazy name is that?" Lyle said. They both ignored him.

"Why don't you ask Ian who she is?" Mother said.

"Because," Stevie said disdainfully, "I'm not speaking to Ian."

"That's something new? It seems only yesterday—"

"It *was* only yesterday," Stevie said. "We broke up, that's all. What's so weird about that? Ian is just a big put-on. His mother and father call him John—that's his real name. He says he could hardly decide between Juan and Ian—Ivan was too Russian and Giovanni too Italian. But he says Ian has more class than Juan, even considering Don Juan."

"You mean you gave Super-Boy back all his T-shirts and stuff?" Lyle asked. "What'll you sleep in if you gave him back all his T-shirts?"

"My pajamas, nosy," Stevie said with dignity. "You just look after your tonsils and let my pajamas alone, huh?"

"My tonsils!" Lyle cried, clutching his throat dramatically. "I knew I forgot something. I left them in my desk at summer school yesterday. If Bosun sees that baby-food jar he's likely to think it's trash and throw it out. Bosun wouldn't know pickled-tonsils-in-alcohol if he saw them. I better phone somebody—Mom, what's Bosun's last name?"

"Too late, kid," Stevie said. "The janitors have already cleaned up the school; Bosun likes a day off too, you know. Either your tonsils are already gone—or he just left them there. Probably he left them alone," she added more kindly. After all, Lyle was only twelve. "He probably thought they were a specimen for science class." Lyle was one of the smart kids chosen to go to school this summer for an experimental project in Special Interests. The trouble with Lyle was that he had about a million special interests.

"Yeah!" Lyle said. "That's right! I'll put a label on the jar saying SCIENCE—if I get them back Monday. Then my tonsils will be safe. Thanks, Stevie. Say, want to see me do a card trick?"

"I haven't got time right now, Lyle," Stevie said absently. "I've got to wash and roll my hair for tonight."

"I'll lend you one of my old T-shirts to sleep in if you'll watch just this one," Lyle said, his blue eyes innocent; but he was getting ready to dodge. " 'Course, it won't smell like British Sterling, but—" Skillfully he evaded the book she picked up and threw. He had had long practice in dodging things Stevie threw at him.

"Where are you going tonight if you and Ian—?" Mother asked.

"I've got a date with Al. We're going to the Emerald Blister with some of the others."

"Where Ian's playing," Lyle teased. "Ian and the Big Kids. Who but Super-Boy would ever name his band that? Even if he did steal it from Rowan and Martin."

"How are you going to get there?" Mother asked.

"We're going with Bill and Joy and Tinky and Butch in Bill's father's pickup truck. Bill got his driver's license on his birthday last month."

"Do you sit in the back of the truck or what?" Lyle said. Stevie ignored him as usual.

"Well, you'll be home by twelve?" Mother said. "Leave the dance by eleven thirty."

"Of course."

Stevie went to roll her long blond hair so it would fall with the curve just the right distance from the ends. Mother was pretty good about letting her come to supper with her hair in rollers when Daddy wasn't going to be home. But when Stevie appeared with her hair wrapped around tin cans in smooth rolls, Lyle shrank back in mock horror. "A monster!" he shrieked. "Save me! A monster! Wired for sound! I can't eat sitting across from a monster!"

"You could eat anywhere, any time, with anything sitting across from you," Stevie retorted.

"What are those things on your head?" Mother asked uncertainly.

"I couldn't get my curler cap on over them," Stevie said apologetically. "The big ones on top are soft-drink cans, Mother, and the smaller ones just beneath them are orange-juice cans. The others are my regular rollers, of course. Don't you think it's a tuff idea?"

"Well—it's ingenious," Mother conceded.

Lyle had lost interest in the curler discussion. He was wishing aloud that the rain would stop before his land turtles, which lived in the compost pile, drowned. Then he had another thought. "Hey—does Bill's father's pickup truck have a top over the back?" he asked. "How about if you all get drowned on the way to that Emerald what's-its-name, huh?"

"Bill will let us girls crowd up front in the cab with him," Stevie said. "Not that it's any of your business. The boys have ponchos. They won't get too wet. If they do—well, they can dry out dancing."

"What fun!" Lyle cried in the high, happy tone of Dick-and-Jane on a picnic. Stevie was tempted to hit him, but it was beneath her dignity to squabble at the table. Especially while Mother was waiting for Lyle to say grace.

He went back to his Dick-and-Jane characterization for that too:

"Thank You for the world so sweet,
Thank You for the food we eat,
Thank You for the birds that sing,
Thank You, God, for everything."

Then he murmured, "Especially for getting Stevie a date tonight so she'll get gone. Please pass the sugar."

"You don't need the sugar, Lyle," Stevie said patiently. "You're so sweet."

"I like my ice tea nice and syrupy," he said serenely, putting in another spoonful and stirring. "Don't you wish *you* were?" Lyle would probably be a comic on TV when he grew up, Stevie thought disdainfully. One like those who do imitations of Gary Cooper and Clark Gable a long time after they're dead. Lyle was taller than Stevie already, but in spite of his I. Q. and all, he badly needed to mature, she mused tolerantly.

"I wish everybody would start calling me Stephanie," she said, starting on her lamb chop. "It's so much more feminine."

"Why would anybody want to be feminine?" Lyle said, deadpan.

"That's a good project for your term paper, Lyle," Stevie said.

"Who's doing a term paper? Don't you know term papers are obsolete?"

The rain had slacked a bit by the time the gang came to pick up Stevie.

"Hey, that's cool," Lyle said, glancing out the window, strumming an imaginary guitar and singing in falsetto. "Picking up Stephanie in a pickup truck—"

Al waited at the door rather than coming inside to drip on the rug. "Put your raincoat over your head and run for it, Stevie," he said. "What's with Lyle, anyhow?"

"Just kidding me. I said I wished they'd call me Stephanie instead of Stevie."

"Why? I think Stevie's sort of cute," he shouted as they ran for the truck. "A real wow nickname. Not like any other girl's name."

"Oh, well, if you like it—" she shouted back. She wouldn't say, I don't want to be called Stevie because Ian called me that. Now it didn't matter what Ian had called her, did it? She wondered if he had a nickname for Morna Ross.

She could hardly wait to tell the others about the strange phone call. "So—how are we going to find out who Morna Ross is?" she said, as they hung up their rain gear in the anteroom of the Emerald Blister. They could

hear the music already thrumming from the dance floor
—at teen-age night clubs things had to start early and
end early, because parents made the rules.

"Ask Ian," Joy said. Ian had got up the combo; so he
was singer and lead guitar. The other members changed
pretty often. Ian was singing now.

"I can't," Stevie said. "You know that. But you and
Tink could, at the first break, huh?"

"O.K." They were as curious as Stevie. None of them
had ever heard the name before.

As they went inside and started dancing Stevie noticed
a girl and boy standing on the side lines watching.
"Why, there's Hope Dorman," she said. "I've never seen
Hope at a dance before. Let's go over and talk to her
when Ian and the Big Kids stop for their break."

"Who's the guy?" Al said. "I never saw him before,
either."

"He must be new around here."

Hope had been one of Stevie's best friends until last
year. Then—well, she honestly didn't understand what
had happened. Hope had suddenly started objecting to
everything Stevie wanted to do. Worse, she had begun
cutting down every boy Stevie even spoke to. "Don't
have anything to do with him," she would say. "I
wouldn't go out with him if I were you." Hope didn't
seem to like any boys at all. She never had dates. Once or
twice Stevie had tried to get her to double-date—because
at that age it was the only way Stevie herself was allowed

to go out with boys—but Hope had said no, she didn't want to. Stevie had concluded that Hope didn't like boys because boys didn't like her. Mother had wondered if she and Hope had had a fight, and Stevie had told her it was just that they weren't interested in the same things any more. "Mother, she doesn't like boys," Stevie had said incredulously.

"Well, don't worry. She will in a year or two," Mother had said confidently. "Some girls are slower to mature than others, that's all. Ask her to your parties; take her when you go somewhere with just girls. Later she'll want to date, you'll see."

Now here was Hope at the Emerald Blister. Great. Stevie still liked Hope a lot. While Joy and Tinky were drifting over to ask Ian casually who Morna Ross was, Stevie and Al went toward Hope, who still hadn't danced at all. Stevie thought, Maybe she's afraid she doesn't know how. But there was nothing to it. You just got out there and followed the rest. Al would show her— she would ask him to.

Al objected. "I came here to dance with you, not with Hope."

"She's O.K.," Stevie said defensively. There wasn't a thing wrong with Hope's looks. She had blow-away dark-red hair and gray eyes, and if she lost a few pounds she would have a great figure. She had on the same kind of striped shirt and shorts that everybody else wore.

"Hi, Hope," Stevie said. "I'm so glad to see you!"

"Hi," Hope said, and she smiled at Stevie almost the way she used to. "Stevie and Al, this is my cousin, Phil Walters. From Mobile." Oh, Stevie thought. That explains it. A visit from out-of-town relatives, and Hope's mother thought she ought to bring Cousin Phil to the teen-age night club; so poor Hope had to come whether she wanted to or not.

Then the word *Mobile* struck her. "Hey," she said. "Let's change partners for this one, huh?" The music had started again and she seized Phil's hand and drew him into the crowd, saying to Al with a smile that she hoped made it O.K., "Catch ya later." Al couldn't do anything now but dance with Hope, and Stevie could ask Phil a few things.

"Do you go to high school in Mobile?"

"Sure. Murphy. I'm a senior next year—and I might be the next year, too, if I flunk math again." He laughed, and she thought, He's not bad-looking. But not as good-looking as Al. Or—Ian. She looked across at Ian, who had put on his Donovan look while he sang and plucked his guitar. Dark-brown hair, just medium-long, and dark eyes. He's super-cool, she thought, and does he know it. Conceited! That was just one of the things the matter with Ian. She smiled brilliantly at Phil, who couldn't guess it was because she saw Ian looking straight at her.

"You sure are a good dancer," she told Phil. "I'm glad you're getting Hope to dance. She never would come with us." She saw Hope trying with Al, who was a good persuader. He was trying too.

"All it takes is to keep moving fast," Phil answered. "It's not as if we had to waltz or do some antebellum thing like our grandparents did."

"Would you believe it—when my great-aunt was visiting us, she asked me how I learned to dance? I told her you don't *learn* to dance. She said she 'took ballroom dancing' when she was a girl!"

"You've gotta be kidding."

"No. It's a fact."

Stevie thought the band was coming to a stopping place; she hurriedly changed the subject. "Do you know a girl in Mobile named Morna Ross?"

Phil shook his head. "I don't think so. What school does she go to?"

"I don't know. I don't really know her. I just heard her name, that's all. I'm in our school band and we go to Mobile sometimes for games and meets and things."

"Wish I'd known when you were there."

They were near Hope and Al when the music stopped and not far from Butch and Tinky and the other two. Al said "Thanks" to Hope and grabbed Stevie almost before she could hear what Phil was saying about seeing her again. She smiled at him and at Hope over her shoulder.

"Hey, what do you mean, dragging me away like that?" she said to Al. "We could at least have asked them to have a Coke with us."

"And get stuck for the whole evening?" Al said. Then he relented. "All right. Let's get our Cokes and take them some. Hope's O.K., really. She tried to talk about rock music. She asked me what 'hard rock' means."

"What did you tell her?" Stevie couldn't have said herself what it meant.

"Oh, I didn't really know. I just said it's stuff that means something else from what it sounds like it means."

"That's pretty good," Butch said. They were with the others now. "But I bet Ian could tell us exactly what it means. Or he would, even if he couldn't."

"Never mind about hard rock," Stevie said. "Tink, what did you kids find out about Morna Ross?"

"Not too much," Tinky said. "We asked him right out, Who's Morna Ross? and he didn't seem to know the name at all. Then he suddenly decided to know her after all, and he began to give us a lot of barf about how she's a girl who's crazy about him, and he was dating her before he started going with you, Stevie, and now he's asked her to the Old Seville Fiesta next week. So maybe we'll get to see her, he said in that snooty way he has, as if he ought to charge admission, she's so great. She goes to another high school, he said, not Lanham."

"He doesn't even know she lives in Mobile?" Stevie said. "You didn't tell him about the phone call, did you?" The band had gone to Mobile for the interstate competition just before school was out. Ian was along, of course, as well as Stevie and Tinky and Butch and Joy. Maybe that explained something—she wasn't sure just what.

" 'Course not. Let him get all tangled up in a bunch of lies and we'll see how he gets out of them when she doesn't show up."

"Oh, he'll think up a good story." But Stevie felt a twinge of pity for Ian. They were all ganging up on him. They had never liked him—especially Al, who had been wanting to date Stevie for weeks. Nobody really liked Ian except Stevie, for that little while. She'd have to stop thinking about him, though, if she was going to have any fun at all. Al was really lots greater to be with.

"Let's take the Cokes over to Hope and Phil," she said. "I kind of like Phil. He's a senior, but it hasn't gone to his head."

Tinky and Joy were bubbling over with the joke on Ian; they told Hope and Phil about it on their way outside to cool off and drink the Cokes. The rain had stopped and suddenly the moon was out, making the wetness glitter. Bill found an old towel in the truck and wiped off the hoods of the parked cars so they could sit on them.

But Hope was troubled. "Oh, but think how awful poor Ian will feel," she said. "He'll find out that we all know he's sort of—well, phony—making up that stuff about the girl being crazy about him."

"He won't find out for a long time, though," Bill said. "We'll be sure he doesn't. It could go on for the rest of the summer. Ian and his phantom date! As long as he's not fooling anybody—"

"But—" Hope still didn't think it was exactly right. "There is a girl, you know. Even if he doesn't know it. Stevie did get the phone call. So somewhere there is a girl named Morna Ross who's interested in Ian."

"Let's find her, then," Butch challenged. "It'll be something to do besides Saturday jobs and rides to the beach. Who is Morna? Where is she?" he sang in falsetto and then went on in his ordinary voice, "And what does she see in Ian Henderson, who's always bragging about his big happy family and his parents who are better than anybody else's and his brothers and sisters who are all so crazy about him—"

"His family's really O.K.," Stevie said. "If only he wouldn't insist on it so much. I've met them, you know. Some of them, anyhow. I don't know all his married brothers and sisters, of course."

"He probably hasn't got any. That kid would rather lie than tell the truth any day."

Hope said, "It might not be exactly lying. There's something they call 'wishful thinking.' It's—it's making believe something is true because you wish so hard it could be true. It's in my psych book— I wish I could do it."

"Let's dance," Al said. "The music's starting again and we got here late. It may not be the best band in the world, but it's the only one we've got tonight. Come on, you guys."

The colored lights were off now and only the strobes

were on. Stevie always thought it looked so great to see just the lightest parts of what everybody was wearing, like a pair of shorts by itself, or just the stripes dancing. There was Kitty; Stevie recognized her pale, zigzag stripes. And Pickles had big white spots on her shirt that jumped when she jumped.

It was nearly time to go. Stevie wished they didn't have to leave yet. Oh, well, she could come back other nights; and she'd get into trouble if she wasn't home on time. She didn't want to be restricted when all the fun at Seville Square was about to start.

Once a year, in August, the whole town went historic and for one night all sorts of events enlivened the ancient water-front square. There the oldest houses and shops of the Old City had been restored to look as historians had discovered they did in the city's early days, and up to the turn of the century. There had been a Spanish period and a frontier period and an English period.

Everybody went to this big thing, A Night in Old Seville. *Last summer.* . . . Stevie had a kind of sad feeling. Not only because of that Night last summer, when she had had her first date with Ian, but because of this dance, now, too. When she was going with Ian, she had sometimes worked the lights for the band or brought them Cokes. But she shrugged and told herself, Forget it. Of course it was more fun to be one of the dancers.

When the music paused, she said, " 'Scuse me a minute," to Al, and started as if to the rest room. She had to pass the bandstand; she just wanted to say hello to Ian, she assured her pride, that was all. He was looking the other way, though, so she didn't.

But she heard someone coming up behind her in the dimness. It was Ian. He took her hand and drew her behind some artificial palms where there was a window with moonlight coming through it.

"I wanted to tell you, Stevie," he said carefully, but not the least bit intimately, "that I haven't forgotten our date. For A Night in Old Seville. We've had that date ever since last summer—and I don't want you to forget it, either. Remember? No matter who we're dating, we're going to meet there on that night every year until one of us gets married. You promised and I promised when I gave you the ring . . ."

"It was just a friendship ring," she muttered. "I gave it back to you."

"I threw it in the Gulf," he said with quiet intensity. "Nobody else will ever wear your ring." His eyes glittered in the moonlight; he looked—well, she was almost afraid of him. "Don't forget the date," he warned, and turned to go back.

"Ian," she whispered. "But—you've asked *her* to A Night in Old Seville. And I'm going with Al. Ian—who is Morna Ross?"

What Happened to Her?

She could see Ian changing, becoming the phony Ian-who-made-up-things. Objectively she watched him do it, because it was interesting to know what he was doing when he didn't know she knew. Sort of like being a spy inside his head—an inter-cranial agent, she said to herself and giggled involuntarily.

That offended Ian, of course. "What are you laughing at?" he demanded. "Morna's just one of a lot of girls who think I'm O.K. When the band plays for a dance somewhere out of town, all the girls come around at breaks and want me to give them autographs. I bet I've autographed a million paper napkins and even two or three autograph books."

Stevie couldn't resist cutting him down. "Maybe it's your pretty handwriting," she said. She knew girls did think Ian was super, at least till they got to know him. He really was an unusual guy—if only he wouldn't be so stuck-up about it. She realized now what Hope's analysis meant: Ian was using his superior attitude, his wishful thinking, like Linus's security blanket, because he was really insecure.

Ian turned away from her coldly. "Never mind." The moonlight barely showed his profile, light against the shadows.

"I really did want to know about Morna, Ian. Are you going to go steady with her now? Maybe we could double-date sometime." She never would, with Ian and any other girl; she just wanted something to say.

He turned back to tell her coolly, "I don't go steady with any girl. I told you that. If it seemed that way when I went with you, it was just because I didn't happen to want to take anybody else out right then. Now I'm playing the field. More fun that way."

"Oh, I agree. Al and I said we'd go with other dates sometimes. But—do tell me more about Morna, Ian. What's she like? Why don't you bring her to the Emerald Blister or the Dream Boat and let us meet her?" She knew why. But Ian didn't. Because Morna was in Mobile, that was why. Even if he had known her, the real Morna.

"Morna at the Emerald Blister? Or the Dream Boat? Don't make me laugh! When we go out we go to real night clubs. The Mind's Eye. The Scene. Morna just wouldn't be interested in a teen-age hangout."

"How do you get there? Does your father drive you to places like that? And do they serve teen-agers things they're allowed to drink?"

"My father lets me take the car whenever I want to, of course. And we usually order a horse's neck. That's a cocktail that doesn't have alcohol in it," he explained kindly. "Then if we want gin in it, I add some from a bottle I bring along."

She knew it was all made up—but it was fascinating to hear him spinning the web that he would get caught in some day. "Your father never let you take the car when—"

"I was sixteen last week." She remembered that his birthday had been in October last year, but she said nothing about that. After all, he might change it every month for all she knew.

"You don't really drink gin."

"Sure we do. Smoke grass, too."

"Rabbit tobacco!" she said scornfully. "Not joints."

"Well, I wouldn't want to be a pothead and neither would Morna, of course. Actually it was just an experiment. Part of growing up, Morna says, is to experience everything and then make a choice."

Everything? Stevie thought. Everything?

Ian went on, "We're off the joints now. Morna says we can generate our own excitement."

"Morna must be pretty special. You must have known her a good while."

"She is. A very special girl." Yeah, Stevie thought. Because you made her up, trying to make me jealous.

"Where does she live?"

"Over on the other side of town. On Perdido Bay, actually. Her father's a big real-estate man. Sometimes he finds a prospect who wants their house; so he sells it, just like that, and finds them another one. That's why she moves a lot. And goes to a lot of different schools. But she's always in the band. She can play clarinet and oboe. *And* flute."

"Where'd you meet her?" Stevie persisted, because she knew Ian couldn't resist the opportunity to embroider his story. She could see him elaborating the design as he went.

"Last year at district meet. Her band won. Remember the girl who played the alto clarinet for Woodman High —no, you wouldn't—but that was Morna."

"I think I do remember her," Stevie said, faking. "A redhead, wasn't she? Older than you? Tall and—well, solid?"

"No, of course not. Morna is small and has brown hair and green eyes. She's beautiful. You never saw eyes like hers."

You didn't either, Stevie wanted to say. "I'd love to meet her," she murmured. "How about doubling with Al and me sometime?" she asked again.

"Can't. Morna says double-dating is childish. You'll outgrow it too, Stevie."

"It's fun, when the others are your friends," Stevie said. "What I think is childish is pretending to be grown up and going to a real night club where they don't want you and ordering a kid's cocktail."

"We're going to get real cocktails next time," Ian said, suddenly putting his imagination into high gear. "I've

got an I.D. card my brother left around when he got out of the Army. He and I look a lot alike. It looks like my picture on that I.D. card."

"What about Morna?"

"Oh, she never has any trouble passing for twenty-one. She's very mature-looking."

"For a small girl?"

"Look, Stevie, you're just jealous, that's all. Why don't you forget about me? Al's really a great guy, and I hope you'll be very happy."

"You're the one who brought it up, following me here. . . . I hope you'll be happy, too. But—you might be lonely." She decided to be the one who walked off, leaving him to wonder what she meant. And leaving him to wonder if she'd possibly meet him in Seville Square on A Night in Old Seville.

Why, it's just a week from tonight, she thought as she went back to Al and the others. Ian'll have to say he's changing his plans about Morna if he really expects to meet me. But I don't think I'll risk it. He may be planning to stand me up anyway, just to feed his vanity and see if I'll wait around for him by myself at the Apothecary's.

"Hey, we wondered where you'd gone," Tinky said. "You didn't go to the Hers, because Joy and I have been since you left."

"I was talking to Ian behind the bandstand. Trying to find out about Morna. He says she's got brown hair and green eyes and is small, but that she looks like she's over twenty-one when they go to real night clubs. Which he says they do."

"Barf," Bill said.

Stevie went on, "And she was alto clarinet in the band from Woodman that beat us in the finals last year at district meet."

"I know the Woodman alto clarinet," Joy said. "Her name's Terry Carter. They only have one alto."

"Hey, we've got to go home right now," Stevie said, "or I won't get to go out again for maybe a month. Hurry, please, Bill! I almost forgot my curfew."

"That's what talking to Ian Henderson will do to a girl," Al grumbled, but pleasantly. He knew she was just doing detective work.

This time, since it wasn't raining, Joy sat with Bill in the cab and the others crowded into the back of the truck, holding onto each other as they rounded the curves. Stevie looked at Al's nice ordinary face and thought, He's not as different-looking as Ian, but I'd lots rather date him. In fact, she added vehemently in her mind, I'd rather date anybody than Ian.

It was no use thinking about the past year. She wouldn't go to the rendezvous with Ian at A Night in Old Seville, either.

Would she?

"I wonder if Ian will still be saying next weekend that Morna Ross is coming to the Square?" Tinky said.

"Oh, she'll break a leg or something," Butch said. "You'll see."

They didn't know Stevie was supposed to be at the Apothecary's, where Ian was to find her as he had last year. She'd tell them, of course, if she decided to do it, and then she'd be—safe. They'd be somewhere, watching. It would be just part of the joke. Ian couldn't stand her up, because she would be Al's date really.

But though Ian's paper-doll Morna might break a leg, Stevie couldn't forget that somewhere there was a real Morna Ross who had screamed and who had been cut off by a rough hand over her mouth.

"Hey, we're not giving up on finding the real Morna Ross, are we?" she asked. "That kid's in trouble. And, when you think about it, she probably doesn't actually know Ian any more than he knows her. Or why'd she call him John at first? And anything might have happened to her—tonight while we were out dancing—"

"Somebody—like her father—might have cut off her head," Tinky said, giggling, "to keep her from getting involved with Ian. Her father might have thought he'd rather see her dead."

"Shut up, Tink," Joy said. "She might really be dead by this time. You're giving me the shivers. It sure was a strange sort of phone call, Stevie."

The truck skidded to a screeching halt in front of Stevie's house. "One minute to midnight!" Bill announced. "Told you we'd make it. Hope your clock's the same as my watch."

"Got to rush," Stevie said. "Thanks, Bill. It was fun, Al. See y'all."

" 'Night."

"Hey, I'm coming with you," Al said.

"O.K., but you have to go right back. I'm late." She would have skipped the good-night kiss in her hurry, but she gave him a hasty one in the shadows of the porch. "Sure I love you. But I have to report in by twelve."

Mother wasn't waiting up, but Stevie saw her light under the door and knew she was reading in bed. For some reason, mothers couldn't sleep until their kids were home.

She called softly, "I'm home, Mother," and heard her mother say, "Good. Have some cookies and milk if you like, Stevie."

She got a couple of cookies and a glass of milk and knocked on her mother's door. Mother always said, "Come in." Stevie sat down at the foot of the bed and said, "Did you get any more weird phone calls, Mother?"

"Not a one." Mother put a card in her book and closed it and smiled at Stevie. "Did you all have a good time?"

"We always do. Mother, Hope Dorman was there, with her cousin Phil something. He was right nice. Al danced with Hope while I was dancing with Phil, but Al wasn't too happy about it."

"I'm glad you saw Hope."

"I like Hope, Mother. The others do too, but they don't understand her the way I do. Hope's a pretty deep thinker; she could be a real brain if she tried. She's figured out that Ian is really pretty insecure."

"Why does she think so? He always seemed to overflow with self-confidence when he was around here."

"That's just it. Hope said something about Ian that made sense. Something from a psych book. Like, all his posing was really because he wished the things he thought about himself were true, not that they really were. Mother, he made up—right on the spot—a girl named Morna Ross, when he had never heard of her before. He said she's a girl who's crazy about him. And he didn't even realize she doesn't live in this town. He said she goes to Woodman and plays alto clarinet in their band. Joy knows Woodman's alto clarinet, and she's not Morna Ross."

"Well, he's still pretty young," her mother said. "He doesn't know how to deal with his girl problems."

"What I'm kind of worried about is the real Morna Ross," Stevie said. "The one he doesn't know telephoned here from Mobile. She might have been kidnaped or—or something worse—after we were cut off. I don't suppose there's anything we can do about it though."

"Not tonight, anyway," her mother said, smiling. "Go to bed, Stevie; we both need some sleep. Maybe tomorrow when your father comes home he can think of something. If he believes there really was a scream that ended that odd phone call."

"If only we had her fingerprints!" Stevie said. "He

could find out all about her, maybe, if we had those."
Her father, as head of the police department's Identification Bureau, was a fingerprint expert, and she thought
of him as almost a magician, the way he could identify
criminals by using just a tiny bit of a fingerprint. But
he would have to be convinced that the mystery needed
investigating, and that might not be easy.

"Good night, Stevie. Be sure the front door is locked."

Stevie swallowed the crumbs of the cookies and the
last drop of milk. "Good night, Mother." She bent over
the pillow for the good-night kiss and hug her mother
reached up to give her.

Taking the glass back to the kitchen and then check-
ing the front door, Stevie mused again, I wish I had her
fingerprints . . .

On Tuesday, when the mail came, she had them.

🌸 The Mysterious Letter

The letter came long after Daddy had gone to work and Lyle to school. (She'd been right; Daddy didn't think she'd heard any scream, either.) Stevie was out in the yard cutting roses for the living room when she saw the postman, Mr. Beavers. The mail was getting later every day, she thought.

She waved her shears at Mr. Beavers and cut two more of the New Dawn buds, which pleased her with their delicate pink that was almost not pink at all.

Then she took the stuff out of the mailbox and went inside. She shuffled through it, looking for a tape from Vicki or Jane or Connie, who lived in the town where she visited her grandmother every summer. They never wrote letters any more, since all of them had cassette recorders. But they were taking their time about answering Stevie's tape. Oh, well, there wasn't too much you could say that wouldn't sound silly on tape. Sometimes they just said "Hi," and "Listen to this," and then played a record for each other. But now she could tell them about Morna Ross and Ian. If they would only send back the tape. They economized by using the same one, erasing the message to record the new one.

There was no tape. But there was a letter for Miss Stephanie Barron, addressed to her at Lanham High School and forwarded in Miss Hay's neat script. Miss Hay must not be taking any vacation at all—working in the summer-school office as well as during the regular semesters. Poor Miss Hay.

She wondered who in the world could have written to her at school in the summertime, when everybody should know she wouldn't be there. Somebody who didn't know her home address but knew where she went to school—maybe somebody who had seen her play in the band?

Then the postmark registered on Stevie's consciousness. It was *Mobile*. Stevie could feel her heart beating faster with excitement. If Morna had written to her Saturday night—yes, the letter would have reached the school on Monday and been forwarded here this morning. It could be from Morna. She turned it over. On the flip side was *Morna Ross, 825 St. Giles Street, Mobile, Alabama 36603*.

She didn't even feel the rose thorns as she huddled the flowers in her arm and ran to the kitchen, calling, "Mother! Look at this—"

She dropped everything except the letter on the kitchen counter and pointed out the address to her mother, stammering in her excitement, "Look who it's from!"

"Well, open it," Mother said. "That's the way to find out what this whole mystery is about."

"I'll just hold it by the edges, though," Stevie said, remembering discussions with Daddy about discovering identity by fingerprints. Morna might just have an alias. Maybe her fingerprints would be important somehow, even if the letter did explain all about the strange phone call. Fingerprints must never be blurred by handling.

Mother went on serenely rolling out pastry while Stevie carefully unfolded the letter, holding only the edges, and laid each of the several note-paper pages separately on the other end of the counter while reading ahead eagerly. Her forehead creased in a frown of puzzlement.

"Mother," she said slowly, "it's just about the strangest letter I ever got. Stranger than the phone call. And it won't help us a bit in finding out what this whole mystery is about."

"What does she say?"

"I'll read it to you. She's doodled all over the edges, but I can read it O.K. See what you make of it.

" 'Dear Stephanie,

" 'The school band I play with doesn't have all the instruments to compete in meets. See, would you, if your band has a *cor-de-chasse* to spare? We can't pay very much—say twenty-five dollars or name a reasonable price. Or how about drums? They are needed and will be O.K., I know. These instruments are what we need most.

" 'I'm writing this letter really before anybody authorizes writing to your band about it, but know they will because we are short of instruments always.

" 'We all enjoyed watching Lanham compete here. Me, I've admired you since the first time I saw you. I called one day but if you were home you didn't answer. I can try again, but tell me by letter what to do if I send check—I mean to what name? Please give me an answer by next week. This would pave the way for the purchase, <u>see</u>?' "

"And the 'see' is underlined twice," Stevie broke off to explain. Then she went on reading aloud, still being careful not to touch the paper.

" 'Our bandmaster, seeing your answer to this letter and the cost, will know what we'll be able to afford. Opened bids are in, as they come in well in advance; so as I'd like yours this needs answering now. You and I both are first flutes, so my personal interest is only for the band. Hope we'll go over there to play and are in competitions together so we can meet.

" 'Many apologies if these things have bothered you. I really never would have written so much to anybody I didn't know, except to ask about the drums and the possible second-hand *cor-de-chasse*.

" 'Thank you very much. The whole band depends on me and on my arranging about it; so will you please give me an answer by return mail and if you and I correspond maybe we will be pen pals. Write to me soon again, and tell me all your band's news about being really with it!

" 'With all my thanks,
Morna Ross.' "

"Now, Mother, what do you think?" Stevie demanded. "Is the kid out of her tree?"

"She certainly does express herself in an odd, stilted

way," Mother agreed. "It sounds anything but natural. Almost as if she were translating from a foreign language. Yet her name doesn't sound particularly foreign."

"It's not exactly a common name," Stevie said. "But it doesn't sound Spanish or French or Italian or anything."

"There's a phrase in it that sounds French, though," Mother pointed out. "Is a *cor-de-chasse* an instrument played in a band, Stevie?"

"Not in our band," Stevie said.

"I have a French dictionary somewhere," Mother said thoughtfully. "Why don't you look up *cor-de-chasse*? I think the dictionary is on the second shelf of the bookcase."

"The whole thing's crazy," Stevie said as she brought the French dictionary back to the kitchen. "She must have saved our program from the interstate competition we went to in Mobile last spring. It had my name on it, of course, and that I played first flute. But it's weird. She says in one place that nobody authorized her to write and in another that they're depending on her to make the arrangements. But anybody would know a bandmaster wouldn't get one of the kids to try to buy instruments."

"Maybe she's the band's secretary and writes their letters," Mother said.

Stevie was flipping through the French-English dictionary. "Why, this is funny, Mother. Guess what a *cor-*

de-chasse is? Here's a picture of it. It's nothing but a French horn. Now why couldn't she have said 'French horn'? That's what anybody in a band would call it. If she's really in a band she'd know that. And—Mother! Nobody in a band would ever think you could buy a French horn for twenty-five dollars! Not even a second-hand one."

"What does it cost then—about fifty?" Mother asked.

"Mother!" Stevie was appalled. "Three hundred and fifty is what Ian's father paid for his, and it was third-hand. They could cost four or five hundred dollars, new."

"It's puzzling, all right," her mother agreed. "But don't expect parents to keep up with prices of things like that. All I know is what flutes cost."

The kitchen door opened and Lyle came in with his walking-catfish carrier in one hand. He had made it out of a large metal canister so that he could take a little water in it sometimes, even though Sport could exist for a good long time without water. He had fitted part of the top with wire screen to give Sport some air. Whenever he went out with the walking catfish he was careful to check his billfold to be sure he had his special permit with him. As he had explained to the class at school this morning, in order to "import, possess, or transport the *Clarias* catfish in Florida" one had to have a special per-mit—which his father had procured for him from the Florida Game and Fish Commission by promising that under no circumstances would his son ever release his

pet. Florida didn't want *Clarias* to take over the streams
and destroy the game fish. But Lyle had no intention of
turning old Sport loose ever.

"Is it lunch time already?" Mother exclaimed. Lyle's
special classes met only in the mornings.

"Sure is. I'm hungry and so is Sport," Lyle said cheerfully, putting the carrier on the counter. "Have we got
any snails for him?"

"Let him eat tuna fish like the rest of us," Stevie said.

"Who's the letter from, Stevie?"

"Don't touch it!" Stevie said hastily. He already had.
"Now you've gone and blurred the fingerprints, I'll
bet."

"I'm sorry. So torture me." He bared his chest—his
shirt already hung unbuttoned—like a martyr bravely
waiting for a branding iron.

"Don't tempt me."

"Who's it from?" He came back from martyrdom
abruptly when his mother indicated with one stern,
well-recognized glance that she expected the shirt to be
buttoned before he ate lunch. "Wow! The girl with the
crazy name. Morna Ross! What does she say, huh? You
gonna let Dad find out about her from her fingerprints?"

"If you haven't ruined them." Stevie was so mystified
by the letter that she was even willing to show it to
Lyle and see if he had any brilliant thoughts about what
it meant. After all, she didn't pretend to be a brain, but

Lyle's teachers thought he was Mr. Einstein himself. "Read it if you want to," she said. "But don't touch it again."

Lyle read it through with interest while their mother made sandwiches and heated soup. "I guess you want me to break the code for you, huh?" he said offhandedly. "It so happens that I know quite a lot about codes. There's a book called *The Code Breakers*—you ought to read it sometime, Stevie. Quite interesting. Julius Caesar used a simple letter-code in writing to Cicero. Mary Queen of Scots and Benedict Arnold wrote in codes, too. I think I could figure this one out—"

"Code!" Stevie stared at him, then at the letter. "Code —yes—"

"Sure. It's got to be in code. Nobody ever wrote like that unless it was for a reason."

"You might be right," Stevie said excitedly. "I never thought of that. Maybe she was kidnaped after all. Maybe they got her Saturday night and this was the only way she could communicate without their knowing. Dad can get their fingerprints from the letter—"

"Somebody had to mail it," Lyle pointed out. "She can't be a prisoner or anything. But she could be trying to keep somebody who reads her mail from knowing what she's writing to you about."

"Yes!" Stevie said. "The somebody who stopped her from talking to me on the phone about—Ian— Oh!"

"What's the 'Oh!' for?" Lyle was poring over the letter with a frown.

"Why, I just realized— Ian's the French horn!" Stevie was stammering again with excitement. "When our band played in the Mobile meet—the time she must have got the program—Ian was listed as French horn. That's what she means—she's talking about Ian without mentioning his name."

Lyle caught on quickly. "Sure. The *cor-de-chasse*. Of course, that stands for Super-Boy."

"How'd you know the French horn was the *cor-de-chasse*? I only just looked it up myself."

"Really elementary," Lyle said kindly. "You were talking about the French horn and that's the only French phrase in the entire letter."

"So go on," Stevie said. "Tell me what else she's talking about."

"It'll take longer than ten minutes to break a code like this one," Lyle told her. "It has to be a word code instead of a letter code, and that'll be harder. If it were letters, I know the frequency of each letter in the alphabet and could guess at some from others. Like *e* is the one used most often, and *ea* is the combination of vowels used most often; so I'd pick out all the two-letter combinations using the same two letters and consider those two *e* and *a*. Then I'd do the same with the other most-used letters of the alphabet, and pretty soon I'd have short words that made sense. I could go on from there to decipher the message. Same way if it were numbers. But this is in words, and we need the key for that. It'll be quicker, though, once we know the key. We can read whole words at once instead of having to spell them out letter by letter."

"How do you know it's a word code and not a letter code? It would be twice as clever to have a letter code that looked as if it were a word code."

"Because 'French horn' is two words, and she hyphenated '*cor-de-chasse*' to make it one word," Lyle explained. "At least that's my theory right now. It's the only reason I can think of for using a foreign phrase instead of the usual one, when you're writing about band instruments anyhow. She used 'drums,' see; she didn't call them anything French. If she's using the kind of key I think she is, 'French' and 'horn' would have to be separated in the message and you wouldn't be able to connect them. If she ran them together or hyphenated them it would look suspicious to anybody who read it. But you get the whole phrase in *cor-de-chasse,* and it looks O.K. to hyphenate a foreign phrase even though technically it's not hyphenated. Also it's more obscure to use the French."

"I guess I see what you mean," Stevie said.

"Lunch is ready," Mother said.

"So am I," Lyle said.

"Oh, don't stop now, Lyle!" Stevie begged.

"This will take maybe days," Lyle said. "You don't want me to starve, do you? Tell you what. After lunch you type me a copy of the letter so I won't have to be so careful about touching it, and I'll work on it this afternoon."

"O.K. I'll make carbons so I can get Al and Bill and Butch and the girls to work on it too. If we all try, we might come up with something."

"Don't forget to copy the doodling," Lyle said. "If it's a code, that just might be important. In fact, it might be the key to the whole thing."

"Mother, after I copy it, could I ask the others to come over to see if we can find out anything?"

"Why, yes, Stevie," Mother agreed. "After you clean up your room. And don't you think you might put those roses in water, even before you eat lunch?"

"I'm sorry, roses," Stevie murmured, plunking them hastily into a pitcher of water. "I'll arrange you later."

Lyle ate his sandwich and fed bits of tuna to Sport through a small hole in the screen of the carrier. "If all those kids are going to be here trying to break the code," he mused aloud, "I think I'll just go and ride my bike with Munro. You know I can't work with a crowd around."

"Oh, Lyle," Stevie wailed. "But they're nearly all in the band. Maybe they'd catch something that even you wouldn't catch. It's all about band instruments. Like, maybe you don't know twenty-five dollars is far too small a price for a French horn."

"No, I hadn't thought of that," Lyle admitted. "What does it really cost?"

She told him. "See! Tinky and Al and Butch and Joy would've known that!"

"Well, O.K. They can come. But if I want to go to

my room to figure something out by myself, I guess you all won't care, will you?"

"We'll try to survive." Then she remembered how much help Lyle could be and smiled appealingly at him. "I really need your help, Lyle," she told him. "You're so much more clever than I am. At things like this," she qualified.

"You'll owe me one big favor," he warned her, but he grinned.

After lunch, Stevie straightened up her room in record time, sweeping everything that was on the floor into the closet and shutting the door firmly, resolving to clean out the closet as soon as she had time. She put the roses in a blue bowl and left them to arrange themselves. Then she typed the copies of Morna's letter and drew the doodles on each as exactly as she could. They were all scribbles of someone preoccupied with music: a scrap of a staff with a clef and a few notes on it carelessly decorating the top and side margins of the page. Lyle came and looked over her shoulder and, when she had finished the first one, he took it and sat down to study it while she did the others. When she had seven good copies finished, she put the original carefully away to give to Daddy that night and called Tinky and the others. On an impulse, she called Hope Dorman too. Hope's cousin Phil had already gone back home, or she'd have asked him as well.

They could all come; Joy and Bill cheerfully canceled their plans to go to a movie when they heard about the curious letter. Then Stevie hurried to make an extra copy of the letter for Hope.

Lyle gravely seated them all around the big table in the family room, each with a copy of the letter and a pencil and scratch pad. Lyle stood at the head of the table, like the chairman of the board. Stevie would have laughed if she hadn't been so eager to find out what Morna Ross was trying to tell them. Lyle was better at this sort of thing than any of them, she had to admit.

Lyle, looking importantly out from under his straight-across-the-forehead blond bangs, said solemnly, "I want to quote you a couple of sentences from the opening of Parker Hitt's *Manual for the Solution of Military Ciphers*, and then we'll get down to it. Hitt says, 'Success in dealing with unknown ciphers is measured by these four things, in the order named: perseverance, careful methods of analysis, intuition, luck. The ability at least to read the language of the original text is very desirable but not essential.' "

"What's Lyle talking about?" Al asked Stevie. "This kid just wants to buy some of our old band instruments, that's all. Maybe that's why she was trying to reach Ian Saturday night, too."

"No, Al," Stevie said. "How about the scream? And how about the *cor-de-chasse*—which has got to mean Ian, like I explained to you all? And how about the twenty-five dollars? You know nobody in a band would

ever think you could buy even the most beat-up old French horn for twenty-five dollars."

"I think I've got the answer to that," Lyle said. "I think she mentions a ridiculous price just to clue you in to the fact that there is some meaning in the letter that isn't apparent on the surface. If the whole letter made sense, you'd have just thought she was writing to ask about buying the second-hand instruments, and you'd have answered that note and not even suspected a hidden message."

"Like hard rock," Stevie murmured. "Something that means more than it sounds like it means."

"Right." Lyle looked a bit more respectfully at his sister. He sat down and picked up his pencil. "Now, let's try a brainstorming session. Everybody try to guess what Morna's trying to say—no matter how wild your guess sounds. What strikes you as the craziest thing about the letter—besides the price of the French horn?"

They all studied the letter silently for a few minutes. Then Tinky said, "Well, I think it's got too many words. That is, she beats around the bush when she could have said it straighter, you know?"

"I noticed that too," Butch said.

"So, think," Lyle directed. "Why did she do that? Because she had to get certain words in. Because they were in the message she was trying to put across. Like that about calling Stevie. Stevie did answer, or Mom did. The trouble is, how are we going to tell which words to skip and which ones to read?"

"Let's see which words sound unnatural where they are," Joy suggested. "Look at that second sentence. It's constructed in such a funny way. 'See, would you,' isn't the normal way to say, 'Does your band have a French horn to sell?' "

"There's another 'see' further down that she doesn't really need either," Lyle said thoughtfully. "That word could mean something." He wrote it down.

"There's 'they are needed' instead of 'we need them,' " Bill said. "And then there's 'we are short of instruments always' instead of 'we are always short of instruments.' "

"Maybe," Lyle said, "the 'always' had to be in just that spot to be part of the message." He wrote down that word beneath 'see.' Then he combined them. " 'Always see'? No, can't be that."

Now, as he thought, he was idly doodling, and his doodles took the same form as the ones on the letter. Except that instead of scattering them around the edges of the paper, he copied them down one staff under the other.

"Hey," Butch said. "That top one looks like— It is! It's the treble staff with the first few notes of 'The Star-Spangled Banner.' I'll never forget those notes—we played it at every game last year." He sang, pointing to each note on Lyle's top staff, "Oh, say can you see. . . ."

"There's 'see' again," Lyle said, frowning. "It's got to mean something."

"Look at the doodles again!" Stevie cried in great excitement. "All of you except Lyle—he doesn't know anything about music. That's the one thing in the whole world he doesn't know anything about. But don't the rest of you see something interesting about that staff—and all the others?"

The Secret of the Code

"I may not know the music," Lyle said with dignity, "but I bet I'm the only one who can decipher the message after you tell me what the things mean. Exactly what do you see that's odd about the doodles, Stevie?"

"You see it, don't you, Tinky? Al?"

"Not exactly," they admitted.

Joy said, "Is it that there's no bass and only a few notes, no chords?"

"No, that has nothing to do with it. I think. Butch, do you see what I see? Hope, did you ever study music?"

"I took piano," Hope said. "It looks to me like the key signature is wrong. At least for piano 'The Star-Spangled Banner' has four flats, not four sharps. Maybe that's another thing—like the price of the French horn —that she wants you to notice, but that somebody who wasn't familiar with music might not have known."

"Right!" Stevie said. "The key signature is wrong. But that's not the only thing that's wrong with that staff. See where the sharps are placed?"

"Why," said Tinky at last, "the last sharp she drew

in the key signature is B-sharp. But in a four-sharp signature the last sharp should be D-sharp. And it's in the wrong time. 'The Star-Spangled Banner' is in 3/4 time. She ought to know that if she reads music at all."

"She probably does know it," Stevie said, "and she's done it wrong on purpose. But what is it she's trying to tell us by that?"

"What about the key signatures on the other little staffs she doodled?" Butch said.

"They just have a couple of notes or none at all, so we can't really tell," Al said, puzzled. "They're not really anything. I mean, not like 'The Star-Spangled Banner.' "

"Look at the key signatures, though!" Stevie said. "Not counting 'The Star-Spangled Banner,' all the others—"

"Did you say 'key signatures'?" Lyle asked.

"Yes. That's the sharps or flats that tell what key the music's to be played in," Stevie explained. "And look! The other four staffs—assuming that they're in major keys—are all in C. One in C-sharp, one in C-flat, and the other two—with no sharps or flats—in C-natural."

"There's 'see' again," Lyle murmured.

"Hey!" Al said. "Those notes doodled on two of the staffs—every one of them's a C. The ones above and below the staffs are, too."

"You're right. That kid is trying to tell us something about 'see,' " Lyle said. "The lines of the staff are E–G–B–

D–F—Every Good Boy Does Fine—and the spaces spell F–A–C–E. I remember that much from music class in elementary school."

He stared down at the paper. He ran his hands through his sandy hair, then stopped suddenly, beating on his temples with his palms. "I remember something else that Miss Jasper taught us in music class in the third grade," he said with quiet triumph. "It explains why Morna put the sharp on the wrong line in 'The Star-Spangled Banner'—apart from getting you to notice that there's a hidden message. And the words 'key signature' explain the whole thing. *Key*—get it? She's telling you that the *key* to the code is C. I'm going to my room now and taking the M for MUSIC volume of the encyclopedia, and if you haven't got it figured out for yourselves in a little while, I'll tell you what Morna's real message is when I come back."

"Tell us what you've thought of, Lyle!" Stevie begged.

"It's right there on every staff," Lyle said, enjoying their perplexity. "It's the key to the whole thing. She keeps saying 'See C' in those double notes on the staffs, in addition to all the other 'sees' and 'Cs' in the letter and the doodles. I'll bring you the decoded message before long. I've just got to check on one thing in this book."

He went into his room, lugging the big volume and his papers, and closed the door.

Stevie said, "Sorry, kids. But that's how Lyle is. We could have told him what he needed to know about music—he didn't need the encyclopedia. But he's got to dramatize everything he does. This is like a card trick to him. He's figured it out, so he's got to mystify us. I wish I could beat him to the solution. But I haven't the faintest idea what the key of C has to do with it."

"Should we read every word that has a *c* in it?" Hope suggested. " 'School'—'compete'—*'cor-de-chasse'* —'can't'—'price'— No, that doesn't hang together at all."

"We aren't even warm," Stevie said dejectedly. "And that poor kid Morna may be counting on us to rescue her from—from—"

"She doesn't want to be rescued from Ian," Hope pointed out, and Stevie thought she detected a bit of wistfulness in Hope's voice. Was Hope's attitude toward boys changing? Even conceited boys like Ian?

"Y'all want some milk shake and apple pie?" Stevie asked. "Mother said we could divide one of her pies. We've got some cookies too, and if there aren't enough Lyle would rather have Space Food Stix anyhow."

"Sounds good."

They were finishing the pie when Lyle opened the door to his room and came down the hall to the family room, with Sport waddling along in front of him. The girls squealed and pulled their bare feet up under them. "Time for his walk," Lyle explained and went right on outside without stopping to tell them anything about the code or having anything to eat either.

"He knows how to keep us in suspense, all right," Bill

grumbled. "I don't know if I'd want a genius for a brother. I might rather have a kid who's slightly retarded —and I haven't decided yet whether that's Jody's trouble or not."

"At least your kid brother doesn't keep a walking catfish in the house," Stevie said, sighing. "The paper said one of those things was seen fighting a dog one day. Doesn't that monster remind you of something out of a horror movie? What if he were twenty times as big as we are? And he might eventually grow that big, for all we know."

"I read that the cold weather last winter killed off a lot of the ones that got loose in Florida," Joy said. "How'd Lyle keep Sport from catching cold?"

"He kept the water in the tank warm by setting it near the register," Stevie explained. "Maybe he let the monster sleep with him under his electric blanket, too, for all I know. Or maybe he coddled it with a hot-water bottle. Weird. But I think he's really getting pretty tired of taking care of Sport," she added hopefully, "and it's against the law to turn him loose the way he did that baby alligator he got tired of. So something like a mercy killing may happen to Sport any time now."

"Don't get your hopes up," said Lyle, who had come back by this time and had put Sport in the carrier. "I'm not programmed for euthanasia. And neither is Sport."

"Have you got the message decoded yet, Lyle? Here, have some milk and cookies," Stevie said. "The pie's all gone, but Mother said we could eat the cookies too."

"I'm almost through. Save me some of the chocolate-chip ones." He went back to his room with Sport, and the others sat and stared at the letter and at each other.

"It's nearly suppertime," Tinky said. "I've got to be home in time to help Mama a little. But I can't leave before I know if he really found out anything or if he's just putting us on."

"Come on, Lyle!" Stevie called. "I bet it didn't take this long to split the atom. I bet it didn't even take Mr. Einstein this long to write that equation."

"Wrong," Lyle said, coming out of his room again, papers in hand. "It took him eleven years to perfect the general theory of relativity after he got the special one, and it took Herbert Ives thirty-three years to verify it. But I think I've broken Morna's code in"—he consulted his wrist watch—"one hour, fifteen minutes, and twenty and a half seconds."

"Well, go on and tell us!" Stevie said impatiently.

"Lyle Barron, M.S.," Lyle said, unperturbed. "That stands for Master of Suspense. Well, which would you rather have first—the message or the explanation?"

"The message! What does she say?"

"I think I'll tell you first how I got it," Lyle said. "She

was telling us, all the time, that the key to the code was C. I remembered that other trick the music teacher told us about: wherever the last sharp is located on the staff, the key is the next letter of the alphabet. You all said that the last sharp on 'The Star-Spangled Banner' staff was in the wrong place—so it had to be for that reason. It was B-sharp, placed on the line that is B. The next letter of the alphabet is *c. C* again. That was significant —and your attention was supposed to be called to it by the fact that it was in the wrong key and had the wrong key signature. You gave me the clue to the whole thing when you said '*key* signature.' But whoever is reading Morna's mail and trying to keep her from communicating with Super-Boy Ian evidently doesn't know anything about music.

"It's significant, too, that everything we could pick out as odd pointed to *C*. She kept saying 'See C.' "

"We knew that. You said that before. But what did 'See C' mean? Which 'C' were we supposed to 'see'?" Stevie urged.

"That's the other thing I remembered from grammar-school music class but I had to check it. The big *C* right after the key signature means something—"

"It tells you the time the piece is to be played in," Stevie said impatiently. "We could've told you that. Without a line through it, it's 4/4 time. With the line, it's 2/4 time."

"I looked it up in the encyclopedia," Lyle went on

placidly. "You're exactly right. Every one of the doodled bits of staffs has a *C* without the line. That's the 'C' she wants us to 'see.' "

"I don't get it," Butch said.

"Me either," Al admitted. The girls just looked puzzled.

"It's a very easy code, once you know what the key is —the key of C," Lyle said with his maddeningly patronizing air. "It's in 4/4 time. So it has to mean 'read every fourth word.' If it were 2/4, you'd try every second and and fourth word. But I struck it right on 4/4—the first time."

"You mean all we have to do is read every fourth word?"

"Simple, isn't it? Once you know the key. You don't count the salutation—not the 'Dear Stephanie.' I tried it and it doesn't make any sense that way. But without the salutation, counting every fourth word, it's perfectly clear."

"But what does she *say?*"

Danger Comes Closer

They were all frantically underlining every fourth word on their copies of the letter while Lyle calmly read the message aloud. With the superfluous words left out, punctuation put in where needed, and *cor-de-chasse* translated, Morna's letter said:

> I have to see your French horn. Can't say name or they will know what I'm really writing about. They are always watching me since I called. If you can tell what I mean please answer this way, <u>see</u>? Your letter will be opened as well as this. You are my only hope. There are so many things I have to know about the French horn. Much depends on it. Please answer and I will write again all about it. Thanks. Morna Ross.

"Why," Tinky exclaimed in astonishment, "it makes sense!"

"Except it's still mysterious." Stevie frowned. "Why couldn't she have just said why she wanted to know? Instead of waiting for me to answer her?"

"She wants to be sure you get the code key," Lyle said. "She even underlines 'see.' It takes a long time to fix up a letter like this one that'll sound fairly O.K. and yet have a hidden meaning in every fourth word. And she must be a real brain to do it. She's probably working on the new letter now, explaining the whole deal, hoping to hear from you that you did get the message. Then she'll have it ready to mail."

"Well, let's answer right back," Stevie said. "I'm dying to know what she's so desperate about. Since she doesn't really know Ian, it can't be just that she's got a crush on him. And 'they' wouldn't care unless it meant a whole lot more than that. But what—?"

"I wish I could stay," Tinky said again, "but I'm due home right now. Let me know what you figure out. Call me tonight and tell me what you write her, O.K.?"

"Sure. And I'm going to get Dad to run a fingerprint test and check with Atlanta and Washington to see if the prints on the letter mean anything. If 'they' read all her mail, the letter must have other fingerprints than hers and the postman's. And maybe 'they' are people with criminal records who've been fingerprinted before for some kind of crime that—that might have had something to do with Ian.

"Oh, well, no use speculating. We'll get Morna's explanation sometime."

" 'Bye," Tinky said. "See you." Butch went with her. The others sat there and thought about what to write to Morna Ross.

"I've got an idea," Stevie said. "I haven't told you yet about my date with Ian for A Night in Old Seville."

"Wait a minute!" Al protested. "You've got that date with me."

"Don't get excited," Stevie said. "It was a date Ian and I made last summer and I didn't mean to keep it, though Ian reminded me about it the other night. I sort of thought I might go with you all and then slip over to the Apothecary's—that was where we were to meet at eight o'clock—and you all could be watching and we'd see what he had to say about why Morna didn't come when he said he'd invited her. And something interesting might develop from it. O.K., Al?" Al nodded—not too certainly, though.

"But now I've got a better idea." Stevie went on. "I'll tell Morna Ross about the rendezvous with Ian, and she can be there instead of me. That is, if she can get over here from Mobile—and maybe she can figure out a way. Anyhow, that's her problem, and if she's so desperate she will. Won't that be wild, though? And we can all be watching to see what happens!"

"It's not a very nice thing to do to Ian, is it?" Hope said.

"Well, O.K., then, I'll meet him too. That'll be even better." Stevie hugged herself in anticipation. "Then I'll be right there on the spot to hear what he says and what Morna says when he sees her."

"That's even worse," Hope said, her gray eyes troubled, but she was the only one who didn't agree that it was a great idea.

"So let's do the letter right away," Joy said.

"Lyle will have to put it into code for us," Stevie said. "Will you, huh, Lyle? I'll write a very short note," she coaxed.

"I'm hungry," Lyle said, obviously enjoying his power. "Let's disperse and have supper, O.K.? Maybe I'll feel more like it after supper."

"I guess it's time to get home, all right," Hope said, looking at her watch.

They went reluctantly. Stevie promised to phone Tinky and relay what Lyle wrote to Morna, and she would call the others. Tink would rather telephone than anything; that was why they had nicknamed her Tinkle when a long time ago she had saved up her allowance to get her own phone extension in her own room.

Just about the time the kids had cleared out, Daddy came home, and Stevie started to explain the whole mystery to him, even before he had had a chance to kiss Mother and to finish asking, "What's for supper?"

"Chicken and dumplings," she answered, right in the middle of Stevie's tumbling words.

"Why don't we ever have catfish stew any more?" Dad asked, rumpling Lyle's hair so Lyle would know he was only kidding. *Clarias* catfish were good to eat, but not very, the family had been told when Lyle first read up on them.

"Oh, Daddy, can't you listen?" Stevie wailed. "This is important. You don't know how important it might be. Just listen a minute and you'll see."

"O.K., Stevie. Wait till I hang up my jacket and you shall have my undivided attention," he promised solemnly. He sat down and she perched on the arm of his big chair with the typed copy of the decoded letter in her hand, telling him again, in case he had forgotten, about the phone call, the scream, and the voice being cut off and how Ian had pretended to know Morna. Then she showed him how Lyle had figured out what the message hidden in the letter was.

"Now, that is very clever, son," he said approvingly, nodding at Lyle. "Just for that we won't have catfish stew for—well, for at least a month." He mused over the letter. "It certainly is an odd thing to happen," he agreed. "And a mysterious message. You're sure Ian doesn't really know this girl?"

"Positive," Stevie said. "And she doesn't know him. All she knew was his name. Daddy, I was very careful with the original letter; so whatever fingerprints were on it didn't get blurred. I remembered you had said you use silver nitrate to bring out prints on paper and then put them through that computer, which will tell you whose prints they are if the person's ever been arrested or in the Army or anything. So will you please take it tomorrow and see if you can find out anything about these? Whoever reads her mail—whoever it is she's afraid of—must have left some prints."

"I'll do it first thing in the morning and call you," he promised. "With our computer it won't take long." She gave him the letter, wrapped in waxed paper, before they sat down to supper.

After the dishes were cleared away and Stevie had rolled her hair, she and Lyle settled themselves at the table in the family room to compose the note to Morna. Stevie had bribed him to do it right then by promising to do anything he asked her to in return. She knew he would ask something ridiculous. Lyle had such an imagination that it might be a very wild something, but Stevie was so eager to get the note written that she would promise anything and Lyle knew it.

"This is what I want to tell her, and it's as short as I can make it," she said, scribbling on her note pad. *Dear Morna, Be at the Apothecary's Saturday night at eight to see the French horn. Stephanie.*

"She'll have to know where the Apothecary's is," Lyle pointed out. "Maybe she's never been to Seville Square."

"Can't you include that in the in-between words?" Stevie suggested. Lyle bit the end of his pencil and concentrated. "Don't count the 'Dear Morna,' because she didn't count the salutation on hers," he murmured. "But we have to write it like a real letter, of course. Let's see now—" He frowned up at Stevie, who was hanging over him eagerly. "Can't you go and practice or something?" he said. "This is going to take quite a while, and I can't think when somebody's watching my mental processes."

"O.K. I'll try not to upset your mental processes," Stevie said meekly. "I'll sit 'way over here and read." But she was watching him all the time from behind her magazine, impatient to see how he filled in the message. At last he finished, and she was surprised to see it was only nine o'clock.

"Here, Stevie," he said. "I'll let you read it. Your message is underlined."

Dear Morna,

Our band will <u>be</u> playing, I think, <u>at</u> Seville Square and <u>the</u> parade to the <u>Apothecary's</u> on this coming <u>Saturday</u>, and on that <u>night</u> I'll ask members <u>at</u> the Square about <u>eight</u> dollars for drums <u>to</u> ten at most. <u>See</u>, they belong to <u>the</u> band organization. Also *cor-de-chasse* price if available.

Stephanie Barron

"How's that?"

"Out of sight," Stevie said. "But, of course, the price for drums couldn't ever be that low."

"We need the 'eight' though," Lyle said. "And I couldn't think of any other way to get it in. Besides, she put a low figure in her letter for the price of a French horn; so she's bound to be sure the person she's scared of doesn't know much about the prices of band instruments. Right?"

"I guess so," Stevie said. "Yes, it sounds O.K. Thanks, Lyle. Now what was it you wanted me to do for you?"

"Oh, just a little favor," Lyle assured her innocently. "But not right now. I'll let you know. Anyway, don't you have to get that in the mail right away so she'll get it in time to figure out a way to get to the Fiesta Saturday? This is Tuesday. Let's see, the last mail collection at the corner box has already gone. So if it goes out tomorrow, she couldn't possibly get it till Thursday. That doesn't give her a whole lot of time."

"But lots of people from Mobile come over for A Night in Old Seville," Stevie said. "It's only about sixty miles, you know. Maybe some of her friends are coming and she can come with them. Maybe she can even get her family to bring her, it's such a tourist attraction."

"Well, get the letter written, anyhow," Lyle advised.

"And I did say I'd call Tinky so she could call the others." Stevie went to the phone and read the letter to Tinky, who took it down word for word, exclaiming all the time about how clever Lyle was.

"She says you're real bright," Stevie told him when she hung up. She brought out her zodiac stationery to write to Morna. "In fact, she says we ought to stop treating you like a kid brother, since you're so bright and since you're taller than I am already."

"Aren't you glad I'm your brother?"

"Well, I'd rather have you for a brother than for a sister," Stevie said thoughtfully.

"You mean you don't like having me for a brother?" he said reproachfully.

"I told you, it beats having you for a sister." Then she relented. "I mean, I like you as a boy but I couldn't stand you if you were a girl." She was getting in deeper; she gave up, shrugging. Lyle tried to look deeply hurt, though she knew he really wasn't at all, because he had a grin tucked into the corner of his mouth.

Stevie couldn't wait to get the letter mailed, so she walked down to the corner to put it in the box even though it wouldn't be picked up till the next morning. She was on her way back, nearly home, when she thought she saw a shadowy figure dodge behind a tree close to the edge of the sidewalk. It was a frightening feeling, to have someone hiding as if he might pounce on her.

But she assured herself she must have imagined it. Why would anybody be watching me? she thought. Their street was a quiet, pleasant homeowners' street, shaded by oak and pecan trees, where nothing except the lavish blooming of azaleas ever happened, not even accidents. Stevie sternly rejected an impulse to run as fast as she could and instead walked—though maybe a little quicker than she had toward the mailbox—up the walk and into the house as if she hadn't a fear in the world.

But when she got inside, she told Daddy, "I thought I saw somebody behind the trees down in front of the house. As if he was hiding and could have jumped out at me. But he didn't."

"Oh, you just imagined it," Daddy said. "If it had

been anybody wanting to—to jump out at you—well, I guess he would have, don't you?"

"If they get you and hold you for ransom," Lyle said, "I know a way to fool them into thinking the money is really in the place they want it put, when it isn't at all. You—"

"Shut up, Lyle," Daddy said pleasantly. "Nobody's going to hold Stevie for ransom."

"That's right," Lyle said, "I forgot. Nobody would want her, would they? With all those cans on her head.

Are you going to wear them after you get married, too, Stevie?"

"Lyle," Mother said firmly, "I believe it's your bedtime." Just as she said it, the phone rang.

Stevie picked it up, fitting the receiver carefully beneath one of the juice-can rollers that covered her ears. "Barron residence," she said. "Stephanie Barron speaking."

"Listen to her!" Lyle mocked. "What's she been reading now? *How to Be Charming on the Telephone in Six Easy Lessons?*"

"To bed, Lyle."

"Aw, wait a minute, Mom. It might be for me. And I want to learn how to be a charmer, too. Let me hear her do it some more."

But Stevie wasn't practicing charm-school techniques now. She was suddenly pale, gasping, "No! What do you— I mean— Yes, I read the code message all right and answered it, but— You—you've got to be kidding. Nobody could want to—to kill anybody—not anybody I know—"

❧ A Warning for Ian

"Who is it?" Daddy had sprung from his chair at the word "kill" and grabbed the receiver from Stevie's limp hand, but there was nothing but a dial tone when he put it to his ear.

"It was Morna Ross," Stevie said distractedly. She was trembling and she couldn't stop. "She was either dialing direct or she's here in town. She said, 'Stephanie? They're trying to get Ian. You've got to warn him. Did you get my letter? Could you read the code message? I had a minute alone and thought I might call you and explain before they caught me. They might try to kill Ian—' I was answering, and then she screamed, just like she did the other time, and somebody cut her off."

"She's probably still in Mobile," Daddy said. "She had your phone number from Saturday night; she could dial direct. But it's quite a puzzle. Why should she call you?"

"She still thinks I'm going with Ian," Stevie explained. "Maybe nobody answered at the Hendersons' this time, if she tried there first. Of course, she can only use the phone when she can get a few minutes away from 'them.' Whoever 'they' are. And now she says 'they' are going to kill Ian!"

"He's not that bad," Lyle murmured with delicate emphasis. "The Big Kids are pretty terrible, I know, but it's hard to believe anybody would smash Super-Boy just—"

"Lyle, I told you to go to bed," Mother said. "Now."

"Yes'm." He looked back and said to Stevie, "If you need any help in figuring out who 'they' are and what 'they' want to kill Super-Boy for, I'm available—for a small fee, of course."

Stevie ignored him. She often did, unless she really needed him.

"Daddy," she said fearfully, "don't you think maybe this is a matter for the police to look into?"

"Well, it's getting more and more like a police case," her father said. "But are you sure she isn't just an imaginative girl who likes to play games with codes and threatening phone calls? Especially if Ian really never heard of her and just pretended he knew who she was."

"I'm sure." Stevie spoke with real certainty. She couldn't have told how she knew, but she had an intuitive feeling that Morna Ross wasn't play-acting. And deep in her there was a dread that she hated to face—the dread that not only Ian but Morna was in some awful danger. And that it was somehow up to her to get them out of it. Because she was the one Morna had turned to.

"Well, maybe we'll know more after I run the fingerprints through the master file," Daddy said. "Go to bed now, and don't worry."

"You don't think I should call Ian?" Stevie asked. "I don't want to, of course. But if he got killed and it was my fault for not warning him—"

"I don't think this is to be taken that seriously, really," Daddy said reassuringly. "I can't think of a single case in local-police history where anybody deliberately plotted to kill a young boy. Except—well—" He stopped, as if he'd remembered something.

"What? Was there one, after all?" Stevie said anxiously.

"Well, it couldn't be anything similar. I remember once when a boy was killed, but it couldn't be proved that it was done deliberately in order to get the insurance. Whenever there's a seemingly premeditated murder, one of the first motives we look for is financial profit: the murderer often kills for money or property. But in that particular case the relative who had been paying for the very large insurance policy on the boy's life was acquitted. In my mind there has always been a reasonable doubt of his innocence. But anyhow, that sort of thing—actually killing a boy for money or property—seems far removed from your girl with the code letter and scare phone call. I don't think you need frighten Mr. and Mrs. Henderson with any such unverified threat to Ian's life."

Stevie went to bed, but she was shivering in spite of

her father's confidence. He hadn't heard the terror in Morna's soft-edged voice. Remembering it, Stevie felt goose bumps rise on her arms. She couldn't sleep for trying to imagine what danger Morna could possibly have thought menaced Ian. She tried to believe he was where no murderer could reach him—at least for now. But sometimes the band was out playing for teen dances until midnight, and then one of the older boys would drive Ian home. When they were at some nearby town or beach resort, it could even take an hour or two. She had heard the band was at My Brother's Top Drawer tonight. He might not be home yet. Would somebody "get" him, as Morna had said?

But Stevie just didn't have the nerve to call Ian's home this late at night and risk having his mother answer. She lay there tossing back and forth, turning her pillow from time to time, and wondering what good it did to count sheep. Trying it, she decided it was no good at all—the sheep she was imagining kept moving all around and getting mixed up until she didn't know which ones she had already counted. If they'd only stand still maybe she could . . . Then she was asleep and dreaming; and in the dream Ian was running toward her and a monster catfish was after him, and she was stuck to the ground and couldn't move. She tried to call Lyle, but couldn't make a sound. She woke up drenched with cold perspiration. I know one thing, she thought. I've got to tell Ian tomorrow, whether he laughs at me or not. I won't tell him about Morna, just that he's in danger and to watch out.

After she made that decision, she slept without nightmares.

She knew where Ian was likely to be in the afternoon, unless he was rehearsing The Big Kids. He'd be at Kelly's on the main drag, where the kids went for sodas and freezies and to play the jukebox and hang around and talk. She called Joy and Hope, and they could both go; so the three of them planned to walk up to Kelly's after lunch. She also told them about the phone call and about the man she thought was watching her go to the mailbox the night before. They agreed that she ought to warn Ian. Hope even thought she ought to level with him about Morna, but Stevie didn't believe it would help him any and it would certainly humiliate him to be told she knew. Too, it would spoil the Saturday-night rendezvous. "I'll tell him I'll be there, though," she said. "I hadn't actually promised to keep the date before. I'd better hang up now, Hope; Daddy's to call me this morning about the fingerprints."

When he called he had some news for Stevie, though it didn't shed any light on Morna's mysterious calls and letter. "There are plenty of prints," Daddy told her. "Many are blurred, but a few are good and clear. Some of them are obviously those of the girl who wrote the letter—they're smaller than the others. I had them checked and there's no record of them anywhere so I think we can rule them out."

"At least Morna's not a criminal," Stevie said.

"The new automated system we got from Atlanta pinned down a few clear ones—a couple of latent thumb-prints on the front of the first sheet and several other prints from fingers on both hands. They're the prints of a man named James Dermott, alias Jim Davis, who has a record of petty crimes committed here and in Mobile, Birmingham, and Montgomery since he came to this country from Scotland a few years ago. I'm not sure but that he's here illegally; he may not ever have become naturalized. His crimes were nothing spectacular, though. And, Stevie, he never murdered anybody for any insurance."

"Mobile!" Stevie pounced on that, though she already knew the letter was from there. "But how in the world could he have something to do with Ian Henderson? But then again—how could Morna Ross?"

"I really don't think they do," Daddy said. "Maybe it's just the girl's idea of a practical joke. The man obviously has some connection with her, since he reads her letters. But he may have a reason even for that. Some teen-agers do get strange ideas, you know. It might be she's taking some kind of drugs and gets delusions from those. And the man might be her guardian, trying to find out where she's getting them."

"You mean, like smoking grass or freaking out on LSD or uppers or something? And he thinks she's writing to somebody who's getting the stuff for her?"

"Could be. Don't worry about it. I've got to get back to work now."

"Thanks, Daddy."

But Stevie still didn't think it would do any harm to warn Ian. And Morna hadn't sounded trip-high to her —just scared to death.

Stevie and Joy and Hope had been at Kelly's for a while—drinking a cherry phosphate each (because it was less fattening than a soda) and eating large sugared doughnuts (which of course didn't count)—when Ian came to their booth.

"Hello," he said, sitting down in the vacant spot beside Hope and opposite Stevie and Joy. He had a Coke in his hand and a bag of chips, which he passed around. Hope took some, shyly.

"Hi." Stevie didn't know how to begin.

Hope said to Ian, "I liked your band so much Saturday night. And your singing— You were—well, out of sight." She said it so sincerely, even blushing a little, that Stevie could see Ian basking in the flattery.

"Well, we don't play bubble-gum music," he said, pushing back his dark hair and looking straight at Hope as if he might be seeing her for the first time—though he had known her since the fifth grade. And he smiled at her, as if he liked what he saw. Stevie shrugged inside. Maybe Hope could learn a few things she needed to know about boys from Ian. At least Stevie herself had.

But that wasn't what they'd come here for. "Ian," she said, "do you believe in warnings?"

"Sometimes I do," he said, somewhat superciliously, Stevie thought. She had recently learned that word in English Vocabulary, and she applied it to Ian quite often in her mind. "I'm a little bit psychic, you know. I have premonitions—and sometimes they come true."

"That's not the kind of warning I mean. I don't know how to tell you this, but somebody told me you're in danger. Somebody might be trying to kill you! So will you please be careful, especially when you're out late at night by yourself?"

"Trying to kill me! That's a laugh! There are too many kids around here who think they can't live without me." He grinned his diffident grin, the smile that was so much more conceited than actual conceit would have made it.

"Vanity, vanity, all is vanity," Joy intoned hollowly.

Ian didn't even hear her. Or he pretended not to. Hope said anxiously, "Really, Ian, you ought to be careful. It might be serious, that warning—"

"Well, dear, since you ask me to, then I will." He said it carelessly, but in his caressing voice it sounded meaningful, and Hope turned redder. Stevie could see her falling in love with Ian right before their eyes.

"Who told you any such thing, Stevie?" Ian said.

"I can't tell you that. But it was up to me to warn you. Maybe it doesn't mean anything—my father thinks it probably doesn't. But—"

"Your father! You mean the police have—?"

"Well, he says it's not a police case—yet. Don't you

begin to have just a teeny-tiny little premonition of danger?" she asked.

"Can't say I do." He was all bravado, but she thought she detected a slight apprehension underneath. "In fact, I think you're making it up."

"No, she isn't," Joy and Hope both assured him. "Somebody really did say that."

"Well, I'll get out my bulletproof vest."

"By the way, how's Morna?" Joy said. "Is she coming to the Square with you Saturday night?"

"I wish I knew," he said, putting on his concerned look. "Her mother said she had a temperature of 102 yesterday when I called. She couldn't even come to the phone. But she ought to be all right by Saturday."

"What happened—too much exposure?" Joy said innocently. Hope frowned at her, and Stevie tried not to laugh.

"Virus, I guess."

"Come on, kids," Stevie said. "We'd better get home. It's quite a walk, and there's going to be a thunderstorm. Look how dark it's getting."

Ian left with them. Stevie slowed down behind the others to say to him, "I guess I'll be at the Apothecary's at eight Saturday night, Ian. For a few minutes, anyhow."

"Good," he said. "I will too, Stevie. For a few minutes."

"Be careful," she said again. "Somebody really might be trying to kill you."

"Barf."

There was a sudden cry of dismay from Hope. "Oh—look—"

Traffic was zooming both ways on the busy street. A big black dog trying to cross the street dodged two cars successfully, but then one coming from the opposite direction caught him. Stevie couldn't look—she covered her eyes. When she opened them again, the dog was lying in the middle of the street across the dividing lines, and cars were whizzing past, barely missing him. He struggled to get up and couldn't. There were no traffic lights close enough to stop the flow of cars, and no driver seemed disposed to be a good Samaritan. It was clear that the big dog would be smashed in a few minutes, and Stevie wished fervently that a policeman would come.

Then she saw with horror and amazement that Hope was going to get hit too. Hope was dashing out into the street, between those whizzing cars. That kid in the white shorts and striped shirt was standing up there in front of the hurt dog and forcing the cars to swing aside in order to miss her. But barely miss her! One swerved just in time.

It took even more courage, Stevie thought dizzily, for Hope to turn her back on the cars coming the other way. Stevie was wondering if she herself had enough of what it took to go out there and help by forcing the traffic in the opposite lane to turn aside too. But Stevie knew she wasn't as valiant as Hope. She felt faint all the way to her toes when she tried to move off the pavement.

"Look at her!" Joy said in awe. "Isn't she great?" But Joy didn't go to help Hope either. Stevie knew Joy would have if she could, though. She didn't even blame Ian for not going, though boys were supposed to be able to do things girls couldn't. Only an idiot would do something like this. Hope was that kind of idiot. But wonderful! And brave.

There were only a few more minutes of the agony before a police car got there—someone had called, of course. But to Stevie it seemed forever. Then they were taking the dog to the vet's, and a reporter was talking to Hope and a photographer was taking her picture, and there was nothing for her friends to do but to stand back and admire her.

Hope wouldn't let anybody take her home—she said she'd rather walk back with Joy and Stevie, just as if

nothing had happened. Ian took her hand and, doing his quiet-intensity bit, said, "I'm going to compose a song about you, Hope," and then he left them. Hope stared dazedly after him. "Do you guess he means it?" she questioned faintly. "One of those ballads like they sing—?"

"Why not? It'd make a great song," Joy said.

Stevie hugged Hope and said, "I'm so glad you didn't get hit too, Hope! I was so scared."

"I was too," Hope confessed. "I don't know what made me do that. I didn't even know I was doing it. But I just couldn't let the cars keep on running over that poor dog. My mother will be worried to death if she thinks I do things like that all the time."

"You don't, though," Stevie said.

"Why did I this time? Was it because—" Hope said thoughtfully, in her analytical way, "was it really because I couldn't stand for anything more terrible to happen to that dog, or—was it because—I wanted Ian to think I was brave?"

"There you go, psyching it out," Stevie said affectionately. "You did it because you're full of the 'quality of mercy,' like Portia said in Shakespeare last term. Let it go at that. You don't have to psychoanalyze your motives."

"I wonder, though," Hope said earnestly. "Stevie, don't you dare laugh. I might be falling in love, and it bothers me because I know what you kids think of Ian. I'm pretty sure it's not all true—but I'm terribly mixed up. And so is he—"

"Aren't we all?" Joy sighed. "Sometimes I feel like I'm living in an electric mixer, my feelings get so confused. Sometimes I love Bill and sometimes I hate him. Sometimes I wish I could go to a girls' school and never see any more boys *ever*. Then again, I get so blue when Bill doesn't call me as soon as I expect him to—"

"Maybe we're just getting hungry again," Stevie said practically. "I feel that way too, when you talk about it. Al hasn't called yet today."

"Hey, do y'all realize it's only a couple more days till the Fiesta?" Joy said. "What a Night in Old Seville it's going to be."

"We'll all go together," Stevie said, as if it were already decided.

"I haven't got a date," Hope said hesitantly. A year ago, Stevie mused, Hope would have said, "I don't want to because you're going with boys." Now she seemed wistful. Wish I could get her a date, Stevie thought.

"Well, I'm hoping you'll get Ian on the rebound," she said candidly. "He's going to be awfully mad at me, and since he doesn't really know Morna, even if she comes he won't be dating her. So—"

"Oh, do you really think—?" Hope said.

"I think he likes you already," Stevie said. "Give it a try. It'll be an educational experience, anyhow. Come on and go with us."

"Well, O.K.—if you guess Al and Bill and Tinky and Butch won't mind."

"A crowd is always more fun," Joy said. "Come on, Hope."

"We can pick you up, don't worry," Stevie said. "I guess we'll be going in Bill's father's pickup truck." She giggled at the same old play on words. "Maybe we can leave early and eat supper there—some of the special Seville stuff like smoked mullet and gaspachee salad and Nassau grits. Then we could hide in the old Cemetery and watch for Ian on his way to the Apothecary's. Afterward I could go to meet him. And Morna."

"The Cemetery's not really close enough," Joy objected. "Can't we hide across the street somewhere near where the old Calaboza was, or even at the Corner Grocery? It'll be open and selling souvenirs and stuff that night. And they're both nearer the Apothecary's than the Cemetery is. Exactly where do you and Ian plan to meet—inside or outside, Stevie?"

"That first time—last year—I was just walking by and he came alongside and said, 'Hello, dear'—you know how affected he sounds with that 'dear' stuff, only I didn't think so then—and we fooled around a while in the old-time ice-cream parlor at the Apothecary's, and then he said, 'Come on, let's go to the Gazebo and hear the Barbershop Quartet,' so we did, and then we walked around the Square, and in the lamplight it all seemed awfully romantic, with the old-fashioned atmosphere and all. But this time—well, I guess I'll just walk past again and, if Morna's there, maybe we can sit on those old steps and talk. Or get some ice cream inside. You all can find a place to watch from—maybe across the street would be better."

"It'll be too dark to see much. Maybe we can be inside, looking out the window. We might be able to hear, too, if you stay on the steps."

"O.K. That would be better. If they'll let you get near the window. Those antique medicine bottles and herbs and stuff might be lined up across it."

"We'll just have to wait and see what we can do in there," Joy said. "We'll be customers—we could order ice cream—so it wouldn't matter if Ian did see us; there'd be other people there too. Or we could buy one of those booklets they sell about the potions the Apothecary made up and sold in the old days to cure everything they had then."

"Ian bought me one of the booklets that night," Stevie said. "I've still got it. It had some sure-enough awful remedies in it. Like axle grease mixed with mashed cockroaches for infected cuts. And oil made from boiled angleworms to cure stiff joints. I'm not kidding."

"Well, Saturday night's going to be interesting, anyway," Joy said.

"And exciting," Hope added.

They were back in their own neighborhood now, and they had beat the storm. Joy stopped at her house and Hope turned off at her street. Stevie walked slowly on, not minding the rain that was beginning to fall, wondering what made Ian the way he was. Not a boy you'd want to be in love with. (Not any more.) But still, there was something about him that made you wish you could be. Hope must be infatuated, she decided. Or could Hope see beyond all his poses to something genuine that Stevie herself had failed to find? She felt a bit lonely, as if she might be losing something when she turned Ian over to Hope—if Hope could get him away from his fantasy-Morna.

That brought her back to thinking about the mysterious other girl in her life—and just as if her thoughts conjured up the contact, there was Lyle at their front door, shouting, "Hurry, Stevie! The phone— It's that girl again—calling from Mobile!"

❀ Lyle Is Gone

Her mother was hanging up the phone when Stevie ran in, breathing hard from the excitement as well as the sprint.

"She was cut off again," Mother said. "All she had time to say was, 'Stephanie? I'll get there Saturday night if I can. I think I can— They want me to go—but we'd better not—' and then it clicked off. But she didn't scream this time," she added.

"Maybe she didn't want whoever it was to catch her on the phone again, so she hung up just as he was coming in," Stevie surmised when she could get her breath again. "But—'better not' what?"

"It's very puzzling," her mother said. "I do hope she gets here Saturday night, if only to clear up all the mystery."

"And don't forget, Stevie," Lyle reminded her, "you've got to do anything I want you to. You owe me a big favor."

"O.K., Lyle. What is it?"

"I'll tell you Saturday."

"Oh, no! You aren't going to— You wouldn't—"

"Nothing serious," he assured her airily. "I'll let you know in plenty of time. It won't interfere with your plans for Saturday. Much."

Waiting for Saturday to come would have been unbearable if Stevie hadn't had something urgent to do. Fortunately, the girls had decided to dress up in period costumes, as many people did for the Night, and she had to make her costume. Nobody cared much which period —the city had historically been under five flags, so you could be anything from a Spanish conquistador to a French pirate, from an Indian maiden to an English lady or an American frontier woman or a Confederate girl in a hoop skirt. Most people dressed in turn-of-the-century costumes, though, because the atmosphere of the evening was predominantly of that era, in spite of the Spanish-sounding promise of the name "A Night in Old Seville."

Tinky wanted to wear the Spanish mantilla her father had bought for her when he went to Mexico on business; but the other girls were making themselves Gibson-girl long-skirt-and-shirtwaist outfits. They were easy to make, and their hair could be fixed in the Gibson-girl style shown in the current magazines, since it had become popular again recently. "I can pile my hair up on top all right," Stevie said, "but I don't know if I can make those little corkscrew curlicue things down the sides of my face—the stringy bits that look like they fell out when the hairpins did."

Not one of the boys except Lyle would dress up at all. He wanted to go as William Weatherford, the half-Indian chief who led the Creeks against the settlers at nearby Fort Mims in 1813, won the battle for the British, and paraded the victorious Indians around Seville Square. Mother was making Lyle an Indian costume but refused to let him shave his head except for a scalp lock, the way he wanted to.

"It would be super-cool," argued Lyle, when she was working at the costume late Thursday. "I'd be the only boy with the newest in haircuts. Pretty soon all the others would want theirs cut like it. Hippies are already wearing headbands like the Indians; they'd go for the scalp lock."

"They'd probably go for yours," Stevie said. "It'd be great to grab you by."

"You may put all the war paint on your face you like," Mother told him, "if you use washable paint that'll come right off—but no scalp lock."

"Well, at least put a pocket in my breechclout," Lyle urged. "Please, Mom? I know Indians didn't have pockets, but I've got to have somewhere to carry my tonsils and my permit. And my money, of course. Put it on the inside where it won't show."

"What in the world do you want to take the tonsils and the permit to A Night in Old Seville for?" Stevie asked. "No, don't tell me—"

"I might need my tonsils," Lyle said with conviction. "The doctors all say they have some function in the human body. Well, mine have a function outside the body. I've used those tonsils lots more since I had them out than I ever did while they were in. To scare silly people with. I tell them that the tonsils are radioactive— that that's why I had to have them out after I took an atomic cocktail for my goiter."

"You never had a goiter."

"The atomic cocktail prevented it, naturally."

"Nor any atomic cocktail, either."

"And of course I need my permit because I can't take Sport without it, and he isn't going to miss all the fun if I can help it. It'll be his first time at the Fiesta. I may think of a way to disguise him as a scalp. And I can use the tonsils if I put some red paint on them. I can hold them up in my hand and wave my tomahawk around and people will flee, screaming—"

"You can count on that," Stevie said disdainfully. "What are you going to use for a tomahawk? Your Boy Scout ax?"

"No Scout ax," Lyle told her. "I'm making me a stone tomahawk.

"I'm grinding it down to a sharp edge on the grindstone at the museum in the Square. The nice lady there lets me use it. She likes me because I know a lot of history. Not many kids even know who William Weatherford was."

"Big deal."

"She wouldn't let just anybody even touch one of those precious exhibits at the museum."

"Will you have the tomahawk finished by Saturday?" Stevie asked.

"Sure. I'm finishing it tomorrow. Will you have my costume done by late Saturday afternoon, Mom?"

"Why, yes, Lyle, I'll try to. Pocket and all," Mother said indulgently. "But you won't need it till about dark, will you?"

"Oh, I may want to go earlier," Lyle said.

"We're all going early," Stevie told Mother. "Around dusk. Why don't you and Dad plan to eat at the Square too, and then you won't have to fix any supper at all Saturday? The smoked mullet is awfully good."

"But I can't stand the Nassau grits," Lyle said, making a face.

"You have to eat some anyhow," Stevie told him. "It's traditional."

"Ho. I bet William Weatherford didn't eat any grits with tomatoes. Even if the Indians did practically invent corn. Maize, I mean."

"What do you think William Weatherford ate? Fried tonsils?"

"Wild boar," Lyle said dreamily. "Roast suckling wild boar. With a wild orange in its mouth. Brown-bear steaks. Flounder stuffed with crab and shrimp. Venison and wild turkey cooked on spits over the fire. Fox grapes for dessert. And never, never any spinach."

Mother said, "Perhaps we will eat a Seville Square supper. But I don't think we'll bother to wear costumes."

"Mine's going to look great," Lyle said gleefully. "But somebody's got to help me put on my war paint in places where I can't see for myself."

"I'll help you, Lyle," Stevie offered.

"Well, O.K. But that's not the favor you're going to do for me," he warned her.

"It must be something gross."

"Depends. Sport and I don't think so."

Stevie was getting more and more apprehensive. "Sport! What's he got to do with it?"

"Oh, wait and see. Nothing he'll mind doing."

"Sometimes," Stevie said darkly, "I think I could be perfectly happy if we didn't have a walking catfish in this family."

"If anything ever happens to Sport," Lyle said ominously, "I hope you have a good alibi, Stevie."

"Nothing's going to happen to the monster," Stevie assured him. "Worse luck."

"Cool it, Stephanie," Lyle said. "Remember what you owe to your dear brother. Remember you couldn't get along without me. Remember I have it in my power to make you do anything I like—"

"Well, why don't we get it over with?" Stevie said. "I've got my costume just about finished. Let's hear what you want me to do."

"Not till Saturday afternoon," Lyle said. "Remember I'm an M.S.—Master of Suspense. One of the prerequisites is being able to keep from telling until the last possible minute. Which will be"—he consulted his watch—"at six fifteen on Saturday night or, alternatively, maybe an hour before your date with Al and the rest of your gang."

"Don't spoil my evening, Lyle," Stevie begged. "We've got something important planned."

"Sport and I will be around."

"That's what I was afraid of."

As it turned out, though, Stevie's worst apprehensions weren't justified. Lyle didn't actually want to come along on the date with the gang and bring Sport.

All he wanted, as Stevie told Al on the phone, was for her to go to Seville Square ahead of the others with him and Sport and, she groaned, "To walk twice around the Square with that thing waddling on a leash in front of us, like a pet dog! Can you imagine—a Gibson girl and a half-naked Indian in war paint with a walking catfish on a leash! He says it'll give the tourists a treat they'll never forget. Like seeing Gerard de Nerval, the French author Miss Ehrlich told Lyle's class about, the crazy guy who used to take his live lobster for walks on a leash in Paris a long time ago.

"When I tried to beg off, Lyle said I'm lucky; when a person loses a political bet he sometimes has to push a peanut around the Square with his nose or eat his hat or carry the winner in a wheelbarrow from the coast to the State Capitol or something impossible like that."

"How does he keep the leash on Sport?" Al asked. "Seems like it would slip off. Catfish don't have necks, do they?"

"Al! Is that all you can say to—to sympathize? Actually he's made a very ingenious harness that fits around Sport's fins in such a way that it doesn't slide off."

"I wouldn't mind it if I were you," Al said. "After all, it's carnival time. All kinds of crazy things will be going on. Nobody will think anything of it. In fact, I bet everybody will say your walking-catfish parade is cool. I'll be glad to come along if you want me to," he offered.

"I'd want you to, all right, but Lyle wouldn't. He says it's just for me, this golden opportunity to entertain humanity. So, Al, you all come in Bill's father's truck, like we planned, and don't forget to pick up Hope, will you? And get there as soon as you can?"

"Sure," he promised. "I'd like to see that catfish parade myself."

Daddy offered to drive Stevie and Lyle and Sport to the Square and go back home for mother afterward, since she wasn't quite ready.

Stevie thought she herself looked elegant as a Gay Nineties lady, with blond tendrils framing her face and a loose knot of pale hair piled atop her head. She wore a rose-sprigged, long-sleeved blouse, a belt defining her slim waist, a pale-blue full skirt with ruffles frothing around her ankles, and a lace-edged petticoat which would show when she lifted the skirt a bit to step up one of those granite street-curbs. It's a good thing, she thought, that the skirt is long, because my shoes don't look a bit like what the Gibson girls wore. Joy and Hope had made similar costumes, but Stevie privately thought hers was the prettiest. Except maybe Hope's, which was pale yellow with black-velvet ribbon threaded through beading around the neck, sleeves, and bottom of the skirt, and a velvet sash around her waist, and a velvet bow in her dark-red hair.

As for Lyle, he didn't look at all like himself. He had darkened his light hair and skin to a shade that he said was the right color and then had streaked himself with war paint in what he claimed were authentic Creek designs. Stevie didn't know the difference, of course, and neither would anybody else except maybe the museum lady who he said had helped him with his research. Not that it mattered. William Weatherford probably dressed like the British anyhow, Stevie thought. If not, why hadn't he used his Indian name?

"We certainly are an incongruous couple," she said as Daddy left them on the corner of Alcaniz and Zarragossa streets. *Incongruous* was another word she had learned in English Vocabulary and was trying to use often enough to make it hers, as Miss Conyers had said to do.

"Triad," Lyle corrected her. "It means a group of three. You were leaving out Sport."

"Do you know what 'supercilious' means? That's what you're being."

"Yes, I know what it means, but I'm not really," Lyle told her. "You see, it derives from the Latin word for 'eyebrow.' So it really means 'with raised eyebrows.'"

"Wonder if Miss Conyers knows that?" Stevie said in mock awe. "You really are out of sight, Lyle."

"Yes, I am," he admitted smugly. "Look at how everybody's staring at us!" He put Sport down on the sidewalk and snapped the leash onto his harness. The carrier was in the way, but he didn't want to leave it anywhere; he had to take it too.

Stevie decided she might as well get into the Fiesta spirit, so she minced along, holding a pleat of her skirt in one hand and lifting it slightly at every opportunity, flirting with an old folding fan of Grandmother's when she saw somebody she knew. Lyle pranced beside her, waving his tomahawk, and she knew he would have been holding up those gruesome tonsils (out of their bottle) if he hadn't had Sport's leash as well as the carrier in his other hand.

On the second time around he said, "Here, you hold him," and she found herself with the leash in one hand

and the carrier in the other just as she caught sight of
Al and Bill and Butch and the girls. "No!" she said.
"That wasn't part of the deal. I just had to walk around
with you, not walk Sport on the leash!"

"Aw, come on!" he said. "Please, Stevie. Just for a
minute. See, I want to scare that bunch of girls—" And
he yanked out the tonsils, which he had colored with
red paint to look as if bleeding, and waved them along
with the tomahawk, giving the weirdest war whoop he
could imagine.

"That's the authentic Creek war cry," he assured
Stevie as he caught his breath. The crowd of girls fell
back at first, giggling and screaming as if they believed
it was real blood, and then surged around Lyle, along
with more crowds that had gathered. Stevie shouted at
him, "Here! Take your catfish if you don't want him
stepped on—" Lyle, recognizing that she had a point,
quickly scooped up Sport and put him into the carrier,
which he had grabbed from Stevie. Then he went on
with his war dance, slightly hampered by the carrier.

Stevie was waving to Al and the rest, and they were
trying to get through the mass of people to her.

Then suddenly she realized that she was hearing only
the music from the Gazebo and the clatter of many
voices. The war whoop had stopped. Lyle wasn't playing
Indian any more?

She looked around for him. The crowd was moving
on; another group of merrymakers was swinging down

the sidewalk, laughing and singing. But Lyle wasn't there. She couldn't see him anywhere.

She remembered, absurdly, a phrase she had read somewhere: *The crowd swallowed him up.*

But that was impossible.

Still, Lyle wasn't in sight. The reincarnated William Weatherford had disappeared.

♣ Suspense at the Apothecary's

"Lyle!" she shouted in sudden panic. "Lyle!" After all, you couldn't miss a half-naked boy in war paint carrying a tomahawk and a catfish. If he was there. Lyle wasn't.

She felt a hand on her arm and looked up into Al's excited face. "Where's your father?" he said urgently. "I saw a man grab Lyle and carry him down Alcaniz Street toward the Cemetery. Lyle was giving him a hard time, kicking and screaming, and the man was imitating his war whoop, trying to make out it was part of the act. But Lyle didn't look like he wanted to go. Nobody stopped them—I guess because they thought it was Lyle's act. We were too far away to try to catch them. But we ought to tell your dad right away."

Stevie said dazedly, "Yes. But what would anybody want with Lyle? Did they take Sport too?"

"I guess so. Lyle was still hanging onto that thing he carries Sport around in." The others were with them now, all concerned about Lyle, all wondering what was going on.

"I told you I saw somebody watching our house the

other night," Stevie said excitedly. "I wondered why he didn't bother me. It must have been Lyle he was after all the time. But why? Let's hurry and try to find Daddy. We'll call first and, if they've already left the house, then we'll start looking for them in the crowd. They were going to eat here."

"But let's tell the police here first," Bill said. "There's a policeman over there." The policemen too were dressed up in Gay Nineties fashion with high, round hats and white gloves and small, fake mustaches. But they carried their real revolvers as well as the theatrical billy clubs.

At first the policeman thought it was a joke when the costumed girls and boys in jeans tried to tell him a boy dressed as an Indian had been kidnaped. But when Stevie told him she was Lieutenant Barron's daughter and that the kidnaped boy was his son, he wasn't hard to convince. He hurried to assure Stevie that the captain would have the area surrounded. "Do you have any idea who might be wanting to kidnap your brother?" he asked.

"No. Unless—" Stevie had a thought. "This is 'way out," she said, "but it might be someone from Mobile. A man named James Dermott, alias Jim Davis. Daddy checked out his fingerprints the other day. He never did anything like kidnaping, though. I can't think why he'd want to kidnap Lyle—but the Mobile angle is the only strange thing that's happened lately. Daddy knows all about that. Let's try to find him—and he'll help get the man who grabbed Lyle!"

"Is the lieutenant here at the Square?" Stevie's father, as head of the Identification Bureau, was a plainclothes officer; only the patrolmen wore the Fiesta costumes.

"He may be, by now. He and Mother were going to eat here. We'll look for them over at the tent." The huge, striped tent serving the traditional foods was set up in the middle of Government Street; the entire area immediately surrounding the Square was blocked off to cars.

"I'll try his house. And I'll call the captain at the station," the patrolman said. "He'll get out the alert. You say the man took the kid down Alcaniz toward the Cemetery, son?"

"Yes," Al told him. "And that's where cars are allowed—we parked the truck not far from the Cemetery. So he could have a car—"

"Right," the patrolman said, frowning. "They might be halfway to Mobile by now. If that was where they wanted to go. What did the man look like?"

"I wasn't very close to him," Al said. "I couldn't see much of him, actually. Seems to me he was dark-haired and tall and big—that's about all I can say. Lyle was kicking around so much I couldn't get much of a look at the man. Did you others see what he looked like?"

"Not any more than you did."

"Let's hurry up and find Daddy and Mother," Stevie said.

The big tent was crowded, and they were hungry, but none of them even thought about stopping to eat now.

They threaded their way along the queues of waiting customers, until finally Joy spotted Lieutenant Barron. "There's your dad!" she told Stevie. "And your mother, too."

"Mother!" Stevie called shrilly. "Daddy!" She got to them fast and seized Mother and started crying.

"What's the matter, Stevie?" Daddy turned her around by the shoulders and clasped her close, frowning hard at Al.

"Hey, I didn't do anything, sir," Al stammered. "We didn't— We got there just as he grabbed Lyle— We couldn't—"

"Grabbed Lyle!"

"Daddy—somebody's got Lyle. Some man took him away. Kidnaped him, I guess. We told a policeman, and they're after him—but what'll he do to Lyle? Will he hurt him?"

"Knowing Lyle," her father said, "I rather think it'll be what Lyle will do to him." He was trying to joke about it, to make Stevie and her anxious-looking mother feel it would be all right, she knew. But she could tell he was very much disturbed from the rapid way he talked.

"Now I suggest that you kids get something to eat," he said. "I know you haven't had time to eat yet, and you can do better if you're fortified with food. Your mother and I will get on over to the station and do everything that can be done from there. Don't worry, Stevie. We'll have the man before he can hurt Lyle."

"Daddy," Stevie said, "remember I told you I saw a

man watching the house? I thought he was watching me, the night I went out to mail the letter to Morna. But maybe he was watching for Lyle instead."

"I'm not rich enough for anybody to want to kidnap my son for ransom," her father said. "And I can't think of any case I've been working on lately in which he'd be any good as a hostage. It's hard to figure why anyone would want to kidnap Lyle."

"Do you suppose there could be any connection between this and the strange phone calls and letter from Morna Ross?" Stevie asked. "You said that man whose fingerprints were on the letter had a sort of criminal record. Maybe he's branching out into kidnaping for some reason—"

"Why pick on us?" Her father shrugged. "Well, like I said, don't worry, Stevie. Your mother and I will do all the worrying—if there's any to do. And be careful. Don't go *anyplace* alone tonight. Stay with your whole gang, you hear?"

"We'll be close to her, sir," Al promised.

"Phone home before you leave here, too, to see if we're there. Don't stay at home alone, either," he warned.

"Let her spend the night with me," Tinky said.

"I believe I'd rather be at the station with you and Mother," Stevie said to her dad, "if it's going to be an all-night thing. Thanks, though, Tink."

"Maybe it won't be all night," her father said. "Well, check with me there any time you like, honey."

"Often," Stevie said. She and Lyle batted each other

around a lot, but she thought, tearfully, that she couldn't stand it if anything happened to him. He was a good kid. She promised silently, I'll even be nice about Sport after this, if only Lyle gets home O.K.

They got in line for the food since there didn't seem to be anything useful they could do to help find Lyle; but when they got the smoked mullet and the other specialties, Stevie couldn't eat. It was nearly time for the meeting at the Apothecary's, anyway.

"Are we still going to the Apothecary's?" she said doubtfully. Somehow, the joke had fallen flat already and now she didn't seem to care much about finding out who Morna Ross really was or why she was trying to get in touch with Ian. Not even why Morna thought somebody was trying to kill Ian. All Stevie's concern now was centered around what somebody was doing to Lyle.

"Yes!" She answered her own question before the others could. "I forgot. Of course we've got to see if Morna comes—because it may be connected, remember. Nothing strange ever happened to any of us till after she called that night. So Lyle's kidnaping may be tied up with the mystery of who she is and why she wants to talk to Ian. Let's go!"

"Let's hope she found a way to come," Butch said.

Bill said, only half joking, "If I'd known how important it was going to be—about Lyle, I mean—I'd have gone over to Mobile this morning and picked her up."

"You would not!" Joy said firmly.

"Oh, you could've come," Bill said magnanimously. "I can manage two girls O.K."

"Just try it," Joy said darkly. "If you want your T-shirt back."

"I was only kidding. But it would've been a good idea. Maybe we all should've gone."

"Maybe we all should go anyhow," Butch said, "if they don't get Lyle back pretty soon. After all, Stevie does have Morna's address."

"I forgot!" Stevie was even more excited now. "I forgot to tell Daddy about that. If there really is any connection, he can get the Mobile police to check that address. I've got to phone him. I wanted to anyhow, to see if they've found Lyle yet. Before we go to the Apothecary's."

"He's only had about twenty minutes," Al said. "He couldn't have done much in twenty minutes, Stevie. But yes, let's phone and tell him about the address."

They found the nearest phone in the Corner Grocery —it was an early 1900s wall model—and got Lieutenant Barron without any trouble. "Thanks, Stevie; I had thought of that," Daddy said. "We telephoned but nobody seems to be at home at that address. However, the Mobile force has the house under observation and if anybody comes, he'll be checked."

"No word yet?"

"No, Stevie. Not yet. There hasn't been time. But

don't worry. The state patrol is on the lookout too. After all, unless the kidnaper stops to give Lyle a bath and some more clothes, he's going to be pretty easy to recognize."

"Oh, Daddy—" Stevie began to laugh, half crying at the same time. "Mother told Lyle to use water-color paint that would wash off, but of course he didn't. I promised I wouldn't tell. But now—well, it won't do the kidnaper much good to give Lyle a bath. The stuff won't come off!"

"Good!" Daddy said briskly. "That will make it easier. Check with me again later if it makes you feel better, Stevie."

"O.K., Daddy, I will."

Down Alcaniz Street from the Corner Grocery they could see the Apothecary's. A few people were walking along the sidewalk, but they saw nobody who looked like Ian or who could possibly be Morna Ross.

"Well, let's go on down there and get a table," Butch said. "I'll say this for the Apothecary's; their old-fashioned ice cream is Wow!"

"I like those little spindly-legged ice-cream-parlor tables and chairs," Tinky said. "Grandma says that when she was a girl all the drugstores that had soda fountains at all used to have them instead of booths."

"Quaint," Joy said. "But they weren't in the Apothecary's in Quina's time, you know. They're part of the Gay Nineties atmosphere." The plaque said that the

Quina House, home and shop of Desiderio Quina, the earliest local apothecary, was one of the four oldest houses in the city.

Luckily the group found a vacant table not too far from the street window, but they all agreed that Stevie had better get Ian and Morna to come inside where they could have a better chance of hearing and watching what went on. "And I do want a closer look at that Morna if she comes," Tinky said.

"At eight I'll go out and walk up and down until at least one of them comes," Stevie said. "So don't order me any ice cream."

"You can't go out alone," Al said. "Remember what your dad said. We'll all go out and stay on the porch in the shadows while you wait. You mustn't get far from the porch. Then we can grab anybody who grabs you."

"O.K. But I hope Ian doesn't see you."

"We'll have to take that chance. Because we can't take the chance of somebody's kidnaping you, Stevie."

Butch ordered, and Tinky insisted that Stevie have a spoonful of hers. It was wonderful ice cream, not like the ice cream you got at other places, but Stevie couldn't even taste it. She kept looking at her watch.

"It's not quite eight yet," Al said.

"Near enough," Stevie said. "Funny, isn't it, how sometimes everything goes so great you can hardly believe it's been all evening—and other times, when you're waiting for something that might be dreadful, every minute seems as long as an hour. I can't even pay attention to what we're talking about. My mind keeps coming back to Lyle, wondering what's happening to him."

A voice behind her said, "Somebody mention my name?"

The Hiding Man

Stevie whirled around. "Lyle!"

She was so glad to see him that she couldn't think of a thing to say except a blank "Where's Sport?"

"I left him to keep an eye on the enemy after I escaped."

It was Lyle, all right, and he hadn't had any bath—he was still William Weatherford. Stevie grabbed him and hugged him so hard he couldn't breathe, until he thought of reminding her, "Hey, you're getting my war paint all over your shirt front—and your face, too." She released him, asking urgently, "What happened?"

The others made room for Lyle at their table; he was welcomed as he had never been welcomed by Stevie's gang before. Questions came at him from all sides: "Who was it?" "What did they snatch you for?" "How'd you get away?" "Where did they take you?" "Do you know the local police, the state patrol, and the FBI are all looking for you, kid?" "Want some ice cream?"

"Sure do. Thanks." He answered the last question first, naturally, and Al hurried to get some for him.

"Vanilla and chocolate, please, with lots of whipped cream on top and two cherries."

"We'd better call the police station and let your father and mother know you're all right," Hope said.

"Oh, don't bother—I called them before I came here," Lyle said, "down at the Corner Grocery. Funny thing— I walked right by one of those Keystone Kops and he didn't even know he was supposed to be looking for me." He grinned and slowly licked some ice cream from his spoon. "I guess they couldn't get the word to every one of them on a night like this," he said.

"Don't keep us in suspense, Lyle," Stevie urged. "I've got to go outside. Morna or Ian might come and go off again if they don't find me there. So tell us—"

"You've still got a few minutes, Stevie; it's not quite time yet," Bill assured her.

Lyle was still being the Master of Suspense. "There were two of them," he said. "One was the great big dark-haired guy who grabbed me, and the other, who wasn't quite so big and was sort of caved-in looking, was the one who was watching our house, Stevie; I heard them talking about that at one point. He was at the wheel of the car, a 1968 Fairlane. They had the car parked in the shadows on the other side of the Cemetery. In the back seat"—he paused for dramatic effect—"there was a woman. And a girl."

He stopped, contemplating with satisfaction the double scoop of ice cream Al had brought him. He dipped the spoon daintily into one side, dug a little vanilla cave all the way through to the chocolate side, and took a bit of chocolate from its depths.

"Go on!"

"The woman was holding onto the girl's arm, so she couldn't have left the car if she'd wanted to—and she looked like she might want to. She didn't have on a costume; she was just wearing a regular dress. I guessed they had kidnaped her, too. But I was wrong. She was supposed to be a decoy, I heard them say later, in case they hadn't got me when they did. Except they weren't really trying to get me at all."

"Stop trying to be funny and tell us!"

"I'm telling you!" He ate a few more bites of ice cream. "The man who had hold of me got in the front seat, still hanging onto me—and I was making it hard for him. But, of course, I was holding Sport's carrier and it was pretty good to hit him with, but awkward for getting away, and then I was afraid of bruising old Sport—"

"Yeah, how about Sport?"

"I told you I left him to keep an eye on the enemy when I escaped," Lyle said. "I hope he's still with those people in their car." He nibbled at a cherry.

"So go on—"

"Well, after the car started I made it so hard for the man to drive that the big one made him stop, and he changed places with the woman, dragging me along.

That put him in the back seat with me and the girl. She
said, 'Oh, Ian—' to me, and then I realized—"

"Ian!"

"Yes. They thought I was Super-Boy. Because I had
dyed my hair dark and all, like his, I guess. And I'm as
tall as he is—not that they'd know how tall he is. They
must have still been expecting him to be with Stevie,
not knowing they broke up. Maybe they don't really
have any idea what he looks like. Anyhow, that's who
they thought they were kidnaping."

"Then the girl could be—"

"Right, Stevie. They called her Morna."

"But why did they want to kidnap Ian?"

"I never had time to find out. I had to do some fast
thinking before they got too far down the Mobile high-
way. I didn't know whether to play along and find out
what their game was, or whether to let them know they
had the wrong guy. If I hadn't remembered what she
had told you on the phone—that they might try to get
rid of Ian permanently—and if she hadn't been crying
and sort of pleading with them not to hurt me, like
there really might be something to it and she didn't want
it to happen—well, I guess I'd have gone on to Mobile
with them and taken a chance on getting word to Dad.
It was a mighty exciting adventure, and I could've out-
witted them, I know. But Morna seemed so scared and
the big guy so mean that I didn't want to take a chance
that something might happen to her—as well as to me,

since they thought I was Ian. So—" He stopped to eat some more ice cream.

"So, what?" Stevie begged.

The others joined in, "Lyle, quit stalling!"

"So I said, quite suddenly, 'Stop the car!' And you know, he did it. It was sort of a reflex action." He began laughing at the memory. "I had no idea he'd really stop. The big guy cussed at him for stopping, but I said, sort of grandly, 'Just a moment. You may want to turn around when you hear what I have to say. I think, from the name Morna called me, that you believe you've kidnaped Ian Henderson. My name is Lyle Barron. My father is Police Lieutenant Frank Barron. My sister and I happened to be together for once at Seville Square, instead of my sister and Ian Henderson being together. You evidently expected to find Ian with her. You made a mistake. Now do you want to take me back and make another try for Ian before the FBI gets into the search? You've already crossed the state line.'

"Both men were cussing by this time, and the woman said a few things under her breath, too. Morna didn't know whether to believe me or not; I could've been Ian doing a lot of quick thinking and clever lying. But anyway, she said, 'James, you'd better go back to Seville Square and let this boy go. He's not Ian.' The big guy said, 'How would you know, Morna?' and she said, 'I could tell if he were.' I wonder if she could? James was just uncertain enough to believe it, though.

"He said to the other man, 'It's probably not too late to get the boy if we use Morna to trap him. Let's go back.'

"So they turned the car around. The other guy said, 'What do we do with this one?' and James said, 'Hang on to him too, I guess. We can't afford to let him go yet. Maybe after we get halfway back we can.'

"Well, I wasn't about to walk halfway home from Mobile. When they parked the car behind the Cemetery again, I jumped on James suddenly and reached across him and opened the door on Morna's side before he knew what I was doing and told her, 'Run!' She slipped out and ran while I sat on James and hit him in the head with Sport's carrier and nearly chopped his hand off with my tomahawk. That thing's sharp! I had him dazed and bleeding. I had to hit the driver, too, when he turned around. As soon as she escaped I twisted away from James—bare skin is harder to hold onto than clothes, if anybody should ask you—and slid out the other side and ran too. After I phoned Dad I came here to meet you all. And I bet Morna's waiting for you, Stevie, hiding somewhere outside till you show up."

"I'd better go," Stevie said. "I think it's safe for me to go out alone now that we know it's Ian and not me or Lyle they want. But still, keep a close watch if you can —in case—well, they're likely to be trying for Ian. But remember to tell me everything you tell the rest later, huh, Lyle?"

"I think that's about all," Lyle said. "I saved my tonsils—they're in my breechclout pocket. Would you be interested in details like that?"

"No, but I would like to know why you abandoned Sport. That doesn't seem like you."

"He might not have got away if he'd tried to bring Sport, too," Hope said gently. "It was all he could do to get Morna and himself away from them."

"I had my reasons for leaving Sport," Lyle said mysteriously.

"Why? Is Sport bugged?" Al asked.

"No—but they will be," Lyle said.

Stevie said, "I'm going. With any luck, we'll be back in here soon and you'll get a look at Morna Ross!"

"Don't let her get separated from the crowd, Stevie," Lyle warned, "or James and that woman—he called her Lizzie—will grab her. And they might take you both, if the two of you are by yourselves."

Al said, "Let's sit over here closer to the window where we can keep them in sight."

"What did he call the other man?" Stevie heard Bill ask as she went out, and Lyle answered, "Mostly, he called him names I can't say in front of girls. But once I heard Lizzie call him Perce."

"That ought to be a clue if your father needs one," Bill said. "Not too many men are called Perce."

Stevie went slowly up the sidewalk in front of the Apothecary's, turned, and came slowly back again, looking everywhere for a girl who might possibly be Morna Ross. She wished there had been time to ask Lyle to describe her better. Of course he had said she wasn't in costume. But Stevie didn't even know whether she was older or younger than they were—or maybe about the same age. The one thing she was pretty sure of was that Morna didn't have brown hair and green eyes. That was Ian's made-up Morna.

And where was Ian? Was he really going to have the nerve to stand her up, after all he'd said? She started walking faster and nearly tripped over her long skirt. Those Gibson girls couldn't have done anything very vigorous dressed like this, she mused. All a Gibson girl could do if she got mad at somebody would be to tap him on the wrist with a fan. She decided modern girls were lucky to be able to wear shorts and jeans instead of these awful skirts.

Then she saw Ian coming, and she stopped in front of the Apothecary's window so the others could see them. He wasn't in costume, but he always looked sort of picturesque because he wore a long-sleeved white shirt—and cuff links—with his jeans.

But Stevie was too keyed up to laugh at Ian's posing right then. Where was Morna? More important, where were the men Lyle had escaped from? If Lyle's being with her had made them think he was Ian, then they'd still be after the boy she was with.

Ian said, "Hi, Stevie. I hoped you'd come."

"I wanted to," Stevie said truthfully.

"Let's do everything we did last year," Ian proposed. "First, let's go inside and have some ice cream."

"No," Stevie said, because Morna hadn't arrived. Then she amended quickly, "Not yet. I mean, in a minute." Where can Morna be? she thought desperately. They must have caught her.

"What's with you?" Ian said.

"Is it eight o'clock yet?" Stevie asked.

"Just about. What difference does it make? We're both here. How many other people are you expecting?"

"Only Morna," she said boldly. "Didn't you say Morna Ross was coming?"

"Oh—that," he said. "No, she couldn't come. She still has a temperature and her mother wouldn't let her come at all. So I'm free all evening, if you are, Stevie. Can't you shake old Al for once?"

"What? Well, not exactly," she said absently. Was that a movement of the shrubbery over by the corner of the narrow porch? Was someone there? Was it Morna? Or—or James and Perce and Lizzie?

"Let's go inside and have our ice cream, the way we did last year," Ian said again.

"Let's go over here a minute first," she said hurriedly, taking him with her because she was afraid to probe the shadows alone. "I thought I saw—"

It was. It was a girl, lurking there shyly. She was pale and frightened-looking. She was a little taller than

Stevie and Ian and maybe just a little older. She had dark hair and—no, not green eyes, Stevie could see by the flickering streetlamp. Her eyes were big and dark. She shrank back a little and then looked with quickening hope at them. "Stephanie? Ian?" she breathed in that velvety voice Stevie had heard only on the phone until now.

"Ian," Stevie said, but she couldn't finish. In the shaded tangle of vines behind Morna at the corner of the old Quina House, she saw something that terrified her.

A man's dark face was looking at them, eyes catching the flicker of light like sword points. A brawny hand reached out toward them.

🪷 The Chase

Stevie seized Morna with one hand and Ian with the other, jerking them out of the man's reach for the moment—he was farther behind the shrubbery than Morna, with the corner of the porch between. They could get to the door of the Apothecary's and inside before he could reach them. But barely. If they hurried.

"Come on!" she cried, pulling them with superhuman strength. "Inside—quick! He won't dare come inside. I think."

Ian balked. "Who won't? What's the matter with you, Stevie?" he said. "Who's this? And what's it all about?"

"Get in there, quick!" the strange girl urged. "He's trying to kill you! Go on—" And she pushed him while Stevie pulled at him. All three tumbled into the Apothecary's in a tangle.

For the moment they were safe. Nobody thought anything of their having entered like that; at A Night in Old Seville all the youngsters did a lot of roughhousing in spirited fun, and hardly anybody even noticed. Except, of course, Stevie's friends.

Some people were leaving the table next to theirs at that moment, and Stevie seized the chance. "Let's sit down here."

Ian started to protest. He had seen the group at the next table, and even though it might be a coincidence, he didn't like their being there. "But, Stevie, you and I were—"

"Hush, Ian," she said softly. "There's something you've got to know. Something I've got to know. Right now. It might be important. And she"—Stevie tilted her head toward the dark-haired girl, who was by this time sitting in one of the little wire chairs with her chin propped on her hands and her elbows on the table, staring at Ian hopefully—"she's the only one who can tell us what's going on. Ian—" She paused, caught her breath. "Ian, this is Morna Ross."

"It's not!" he cried incredulously. "You're putting me on! You're making it up! There's not any—Morna Ross—" Then he caught himself and retreated, his defenses down. "There couldn't be two—girls with that name—" he mumbled.

"No, there couldn't," Stevie said. "This is the one and only Morna, Ian."

"Ian," Morna said gently. "Ian, look at me." He was looking down at the table as if he would never be able to face anybody again. Then slowly, as if her voice compelled him, he raised his eyes until he was looking straight into hers. And Stevie gasped. Why, they were the same eyes! Ian and Morna—looked alike—

"Ian," Morna was saying with a kind of aching tenderness, "I'm your only sister. Your half sister."

Ian said blankly, "No. I have four sisters. And two brothers."

"You and I had the same mother," Morna went on, as if he hadn't denied her. "Margaret Ross. Oh, I know you never heard of her—or me. You don't know your real name is Hughie Ross."

"No," Ian stammered again.

"I was already two years old when our mother married your father, Hugh Ross; my own father was dead. Three months after you were born, your father and our mother were both killed in the same car accident. Even though I wasn't Hugh Ross's own daughter, his younger brother, Malcolm Ross, adopted me. Because his wife had always wanted a girl. But you really are Hughie Ross, Ian. They let somebody else adopt you—the Hendersons. But I didn't find that out till just a little while ago."

"Adopt!" Ian said with difficulty, but stubbornly. "No—I'm not adopted. You've got it all wrong. I'm not any Hugh Ross's son. I'm John Henderson's son. My name's John Henderson. I just use Ian for the band. I'm John Henderson—" he insisted wildly.

He didn't meet Stevie's eyes, and suddenly she was very sorry for him. His protesting indicated, she guessed, that he really already knew, even if he didn't know the name Ross. But for some strange reason he couldn't bear for anyone else to know he was adopted. She understood in a way. *He thinks we'd look down on him for it,* she thought, *when we wouldn't at all. Some mothers and fathers have kids because they want them, and some mothers and fathers adopt kids because they want them. There's not that much difference. And I'll tell him if he'll let me.*

But then she saw Hope looking at Ian from the other table, and there was such sympathy in Hope's face that she amended it to, *Maybe I'll let Hope tell him.* Hope had realized Ian's trouble was that he felt insecure, even though she didn't know why.

But Ian wasn't going to let anybody feel sorry for him. Suddenly he bolted from his chair. "No—it's not true—" he was muttering as he stumbled blindly for the door. Stevie suspected he was crying—at least inside if not openly.

"Catch him!" Morna said urgently. "He mustn't go out there! They'll get him and they'll kill him, I tell you—"

"Come on, kids!" Stevie cried to Al and the others. "Let's catch Ian. And keep close to Morna and don't let them get near her either. Morna's got to explain things to him. And to us too," she added, because the whole thing was getting to be more of a puzzle than ever. "These are my friends," she said over her shoulder to Morna.

But she didn't have time to wonder why Ian's being

Morna's half brother should make anybody want to kill him. She was too busy trying to overtake him as the whole crowd ran, the girls tripping on their long dresses, up the street toward the gaiety in the Square.

Lyle suddenly shouted, "It's him! It's the big dark guy! He's after Ian!"

"Where?" Stevie panted. "Where do you see him, Lyle?"

"Between us and Ian—there! See him?"

"I see him," Morna said. "It's James, all right. Perce is behind him."

"Let's get to Ian before they do," Bill said to Al. "We'll run across the Square while Ian's running around it. Butch, you take care of the girls and meet us at the truck. You know where we parked it. We'll get Ian into it, and as soon as you get there with the girls we'll scratch off."

"Right," Al said, and the two sprinted ahead. They could go faster when they weren't held up by the Gibson girls. Stevie wanted to take off her long skirt and petticoat, but she didn't dare. If only I had shorts on under them, she thought.

"They didn't even wait for me to say O.K.," Butch grumbled.

"Now Ian's doubling back," Lyle said excitedly. "He's going toward the Cemetery."

"Where's the truck exactly?" Stevie asked Butch. She was out of breath, running to keep up with his long legs.

"Right down on Alcaniz past the Cemetery. That was as close as they'd let us park it."

"Hey!" Lyle said. "You parked right where they parked! Or nearly, anyhow."

"I was afraid that was how it was. Let's hurry so we'll be in the truck, ready to go. Bill forgot to give me the key, or I could've warmed it up."

They were hurrying and now were almost in the shadows that fell across the street from the trees in the Cemetery. "Watch out," Morna begged. "They might have somebody else in there to grab us."

"Let them try it," Butch said menacingly. "I can take care of them."

"He could, too," Stevie told Morna. "He's been taking judo."

"So why don't you get him?" shrieked Lyle, as Ian came running toward them, followed closely by the dark man.

"So I will!" Butch shouted. Ian dashed past and Butch launched his bulk against James's legs. They tangled on the ground while Al and Bill raced ahead to overtake Ian. With the others, they hurried Ian into the truck, the girls' skirts hampering their own efforts to get in. Bill, with Joy beside him, took the wheel and revved up the motor, waiting for Al and Butch. Al had gone back to help Butch in the scramble with James, and now Perce too; but James knew when he was about to lose his quarry. He shook the boys off at last and ran for his own car, shouting, "After them! He's getting away—" Perce followed him.

As soon as Butch and Al had leaped into the truck, Bill scratched off. Close behind him as he swung around the corner was the '68 Fairlane. "This truck wasn't exactly built for speed," he complained above the roar the wind made. The others in back could barely hear what he shouted. "But we're going over sixty. Maybe some policeman will stop us. Or them."

"Their car isn't too fast either," Morna said. "It's no good—it's always breaking down."

"Hey, here's an idea," Lyle said to Bill at the top of his voice. "Let's lead them in a roundabout way back to the Square, where nobody's supposed to take a car tonight, and then they'll be sure to be stopped. And in case we're stopped ourselves, we'll be safe from them. Don't worry," he assured Bill very loudly, "you won't get a ticket as long as I tell them who I am."

Stevie thought, Lyle's getting back to his brat status fast after being a hero for all of an hour.

"Not bad," Bill shouted back. "Here we go then."

He swerved around another corner, and the kids held onto each other and the sides of the truck, shrieking as Morna nearly fell out.

"Don't lose her," begged Tinky. "She hasn't had time to tell us what this is all about yet."

"Don't bother," Ian muttered. "I don't want to hear any more lies from her."

"I'm sorry, Ian," Morna said softly. "I'm sorry if you don't like what's true. But it is true. And you might be glad, really, when you know all about it." Then Bill turned another corner on two wheels and she couldn't go on right then, though Stevie could hardly wait.

"That is," Morna said, shivering in spite of the hot weather, "if James doesn't kill you first. I heard him tell Lizzie he had to get you. That's why I had to try to warn you," she went on hurriedly, with the others breathlessly waiting for each word.

"Watch the tree!" Bill yelled. An overhanging tree limb nearly swept off the kids in the open bed of the truck as it sped around toward the Cemetery again.

"Look out!" Joy screamed. "There they are— They took a short cut—"

The other car had swung in front of them and was now alongside, trying to force the truck to the side of the street before they reached the roped-off area forbidden to cars. Bill grimly set his jaw and refused to be forced. The girls screamed as the car sideswiped the truck with a grinding sound, jarring them all with the bump and shoving the truck into the curb.

"He's got us," Morna said in despair as the truck gasped and stalled.

❀ The Other Girl

Bill was trying desperately to start the motor again while the others shrilled excited advice. He's flooding it, Stevie thought in terror, and here come James and Perce after Ian.

Yes. The two men had left the woman at the wheel of their car to turn it around while they ran toward the pickup truck. She already had it facing the other way —toward Mobile and their getaway—when James and Perce arrived at the tail gate and confronted the kids, who had closed in around Ian and Morna.

"You can't have him," Stevie said flatly.

Morna said from behind Stevie, "James, you had better get away while you can. Her father is a police lieutenant, and you kidnaped her brother and crossed a state line before you turned back with him. The FBI is after you. Anything you might get by killing Ian wouldn't do you any good in the Federal penitentiary."

"Now whatever made you think I'd be wanting to kill the lad?" James asked slyly. "I merely want to help him, that's all. I'm his next of kin if his uncle dies, as he's likely to any minute now. And I'm his natural guardian. I simply want to get the lad to come with me while I persuade him that he wants to live with me and Lizzie at Rossholm instead of where he is now—"

"You're wrong, James." Morna stood up to him bravely. "You're not his next of kin. I am. And I know what kind of 'persuading' you'd do. He's not going anywhere with you."

"Do I have to take the lad by force?" James said. "I wouldn't like to have to hurt any of you nice lads and lassies—" Stevie heard the echo of her father's voice saying, *The murderer often kills for money or property* . . .

"So stand aside, please," James went on, "while I get young Hughie to go with his blood relative back to Scotland—"

"Scotland!" Stevie gasped. Absurdly, all she could think of in this crucial moment was that Ian was a Scottish name, and "John" had chosen it without knowing he was Scottish.

"Aye, Scotland," James said. Perce nodded every time James spoke, like a wobble toy when somebody touched its head.

"He's putting on that Scottish accent," Morna said scornfully. "He talks just like anybody else when he's not trying to impress Ian."

"You shut up or I'll—" His hand closed into a fist; his scowl at her was fierce.

Lyle leaped in front of Stevie and Morna, yanking his tonsils out of his breechclout. "Stand back if you don't want to die a horrible death!" he warned in the lowest, most sinister tone he could manage.

James instinctively fell back. Perce jumped back even farther. "What's that?"

The thing in Lyle's hand did look horrible, Stevie thought, especially if you had no idea what it was or that it wasn't covered with real blood. "Tonsils of birth-strangled babe," Lyle chanted, slightly altering the witches' song in *Macbeth*, which he'd studied in the special Advanced English class. "A witch's curse. What's more, they're radioactive. I had an atomic cocktail just before I had them out. Don't get too close to them or you'll regret it the rest of your—exceedingly short—life!"

James looked at him warily. Stevie could tell he knew it wasn't so, but he wasn't quite sure how to handle Lyle, who had tomahawked him and bested him once before. But at least the diversion gave them some time. Perce looked as if he believed it, though.

Then Hope saw a police car, and like an idiot, blew it. "The police! They're going to rescue us!"

James glanced over his shoulder and saw the police car coming from the direction of the Square—the only cars allowed there were the squad cars. He cursed and ran for his Fairlane, Perce following just in time. They peeled out. The police car took off after them—maybe

because they were speeding? Stevie sighed with relief. Well, everything would be all right now.

"I can't wait another minute to find out why he wanted Ian," Tinky said to Morna. "Please—"

"Ian, aren't you curious?" Joy said. Ian was sitting dejectedly on the floor of the truck. Joy and Bill had come around from the cab to join the others.

"No," Ian muttered. "Because it's not true. I'm not any Hughie Ross. I don't want to hear anything about it."

Hope sat down beside him but she didn't say a word. She smoothed the long folds of her skirt around her knees and rested her chin on her arms across them, listening.

"It's a long story," Morna said, "but I'll make it as short as I can. I didn't know I ever had a brother until recently. A few years ago, James Dermott showed up at Uncle Malcolm's with his wife Lizzie and that man Perce and just moved in on us. I don't know why they let him, except that Uncle Malcolm was too sick to care —he's in the hospital now and hasn't much longer to live. Aunt Alison didn't want to worry Uncle any more than she could help; and at first they thought of James as 'family,' I guess.

"For a long time I didn't know why James came there. Then I accidentally overheard something that made me curious. Your father, Hughie—I mean Ian—was the oldest of a family of three. He and Uncle Malcolm had a sister named Elspeth, and James is her son, or claims to be. In Scotland there's a big estate called Rossholm that belonged to the Rosses from 'way back, but there were about a dozen heirs to it before your father; so the American Rosses never thought anything about it. But some of the heirs were killed in World War II, and six of those living were killed in the same airplane crash about five years ago. The last one left, an old man named Alan Ross, died just before James came to the States.

"If your father were alive, he'd now be the heir to Rossholm. By the Scottish laws of something—"

"Primogeniture," Lyle said.

"That's it! By that whatever-it-is, the estate is entailed to the male heirs, as long as there are any. That means it's inherited by the oldest son of the oldest son, on down the line. So Ian is the heir now. I never would have been, of course, not being a Ross at all, besides not being a male. But if Ian couldn't be found, or had died, then Uncle Malcolm, as the next oldest brother, would inherit. Only after he died would the male heirs of his sister get a chance at the estate. James wasn't worried about Uncle Malcolm—he figured he'd die soon anyway.

"But he was worried about Hugh's son; the lawyers were trying to trace Hughie, though from Scotland they weren't making much progress. Uncle Malcolm wouldn't tell James who had adopted his brother's baby. So long as James couldn't prove you were dead, Ian, he couldn't do a thing about claiming the estate after Uncle Malcolm's death. And Uncle didn't want the estate enough to bother to claim it; he didn't think it was worth claiming, or else he might have wanted you to have it. He said it was just a moldy falling-down old castle, eaten up by taxes. Aunt Alison told me all this later, when I started trying to find you, Ian, because James kept after Uncle Malcolm so much about it. The estate must be worth a lot more than Uncle thinks, or James wouldn't be so anxious to get it; and he's been in Scotland to see it.

"I heard James pestering Uncle Malcolm and discovered I had had a brother. So I went to the courthouse to try to find out who had adopted you, but they said they never give out such information, and anyway those particular records were lost. I was glad, because that meant that James couldn't find out, either."

"Why wouldn't your uncle tell you and let you try to find your brother?" Stevie asked.

"Aunt Alison didn't want me to bother him about it. He really was awfully sick. But when I asked her, she did tell me all she knew about it. That was that some people my father knew, a Mr. and Mrs. John Henderson, had adopted Hughie when he was three months old. They were pleased with his looks and, because they were dark-haired, they thought he might grow up to look like their other children. Aunt Alison didn't know where they had gone when they moved from Mobile.

"Of course, it's a common name, and it didn't seem likely that I could ever find the right Hendersons. Or that the lawyers could, either. But when I saw 'Ian Henderson' on that band program—I didn't notice it while you all were still in town, worse luck—and realized that 'Ian' is the Scottish name for 'John'—well, there was no logical reason to think he might be my brother, but I was reaching for any hope. When I showed it to Aunt Alison, she agreed to ask Uncle Malcolm if he knew whether that was where the Hendersons who had adopted Hughie had moved to. He said it probably was—he thought so—he couldn't be sure.

"Anyhow, when I found out from the Information operator how to call the John Hendersons, and Mrs. Henderson said John was her son, I felt sure."

"It must have been fate," Tinky said, "that made you notice the name on the band program."

"Yes," Morna said. "I believe it was. A sign, like. But James overheard me that night I called the Hendersons and afterward tried Stephanie's number because Mrs. Henderson thought Ian might be there. James cut me off and then later, when the telephone bill arrived, he found out where the call was placed to. And so he knew about Stephanie and he got her address from the phone number—there's a book that tells that, but of course I couldn't get to it, and he could, somehow. I suppose he guessed that Stephanie was Ian's girl after he heard me mention the name the second time I called, and he cut me off. Anyway, I heard him tell Lizzie that he was going to get Ian when he went out with Stephanie. But, of course, when I wrote the code letter that same night, I didn't know he'd ever know Stephanie's name or address."

"It's a good joke on him," Stevie said, "because we weren't going out together at all by then. But it explains the man watching our house—and kidnaping Lyle because he was with me."

"I'm the lucky guy," Al said. "He might have caught me with Stevie 'most any time."

"James and Lizzie watched me and Aunt Alison all the time," Morna went on, "so neither of us could call you or the Hendersons, except those two other times I managed to reach you and to say a few words before James got to me. I couldn't write to Ian either because James read all my mail. That's why I had to try to get in touch with Ian by writing to Stephanie, hoping she'd catch on to the code because she knows about music and James doesn't know the first thing about it. James hadn't yet found out who Stephanie was when he read my letter, and of course he thought it was harmless, because of the code. James isn't very bright."

Lyle said, "It was a clever code, Morna."

"Thanks. But I slipped up—he found Stephanie's answer and saw how I'd underlined every fourth word. So he decided to let me come tonight and see the French horn. He didn't know it meant Ian, but I guess he thought Ian might be with Stephanie. I tried to call her and change the meeting place but he caught me. It was too late then—and since he knew I was trying something—"

"But I didn't know any of that," Stevie said. "I thought since Lyle said you got away from them that we ought to meet you as planned."

"Of course. I'm glad you did, too. And oh, yes, Lyle— I forgot to thank you for helping me escape," Morna said.

"Any time. It was a pleasure to outwit old James," Lyle assured her. "And I think we've got him this time too," he added.

"You mean Daddy and the police will catch him?" Stevie said.

"Somebody sure will. He's breaking the law every minute he's in the car, even if it's standing still."

"What do you mean?"

But Morna was talking again, and she had to wait for Lyle's explanation till later.

"I was hoping to get over here to meet you at eight at the Apothecary's. I met the postman every day so that James couldn't keep me from seeing any letters, although he always read everything that came, anyway. If only I hadn't underlined the words in that note from Stephanie! I meant to burn it right then, or I never would have marked it. But Aunt Alison called me to help her with Uncle Malcolm, and I forgot to go back and do it.

"I was going to slip away and come on the bus, if there wasn't any other way. Aunt Alison was willing to give me the money and to help me get out. She agreed that it was the best way and that we really had to find Hughie and somehow get him and the lawyers together about the estate. She said she was afraid if James got to him first, he might arrange for an 'accident' to happen to Hughie, and fix it some way so that his body'd be found and it would be known he was Hugh Ross's son as well as John Henderson's adopted son. Then James could go back to Scotland when Uncle Malcolm died and he would be heir to the estate. Except I wouldn't have let him get away with it!" she said with emphasis. "I'd have told somebody about it. He'd have had to kill me too!"

Ian had lifted his head and was looking at her now, and Stevie thought, Maybe he'll see how great she is, doing all she was trying to do for him.

But still he said doggedly, "I'm not Hughie Ross. I'm John Henderson. Can't you get it through your heads, all of you? I'm not adopted! Nobody can prove I am. So you can just let that bummer have the moldy old castle in Scotland. My family won't let him bother me. My brother will rip him off—"

Then he suddenly put his dark head down on his folded arms, and they couldn't see his face.

Morna finished, "Then James made me come with them tonight, because of the note. But he left me in the car with Lizzie while he went to the Square ahead of time and saw a boy with Stephanie and thought it was Ian—and you know the rest." She drew a deep breath.

Stevie realized Hope couldn't bear to see Ian feeling so miserable when Hope stood up suddenly and said, "Why don't we all walk on down to the Apothecary's again and eat some more ice cream? Just to celebrate our escape and all."

"Good idea," Stevie seconded, and the boys jumped out first and handed down the girls in their long skirts. But Hope, who was last except for Ian, shook her head, waving them on, and Stevie was suddenly reminded of the afternoon Hope had stood protectively in front of the hurt dog in the middle of traffic on a busy street.

"Come on," Stevie said to the others. "They'll come later."

Hope came later, but Ian didn't.

"He's gone home," she explained to the others. "But it's all right. He wants to see you tomorrow," she told Morna. "I mean he really wants to. To hear about his father and mother and family. He didn't even know that his parents had died. He was thinking all the time that his father and mother were the ones who didn't want him—who gave him away to be adopted—and he felt rejected. That was why he felt so awful about being adopted. But he can take the idea that it was only an uncle."

"Oh, but he mustn't feel hard toward Uncle Malcolm

and Aunt Alison," Morna said in distress. "They loved him. They really couldn't afford to keep us both. And they weren't very well, even then. They couldn't take care of a three-month-old baby."

Hope went on, "He understands now. I told him it's better to be adopted than—well, than to have divorced parents, for instance. Some kids have two parents, some have four, some even have six, and some have adopted parents. So what? He had been thinking all his life it was a big deal to be adopted, see? He was afraid, since none of the rest of us were, that we'd make something of it. All he wanted was to belong—to belong to the Hendersons, and to keep any of us from knowing he didn't really. He wanted terribly to be able to say 'we' and know it really was 'we.' But I showed him how great it is to have a real sister who wants so to be his sister that she went to all that trouble to find him." She smiled shyly at Morna, and Morna smiled back, a beautiful smile, like Ian's Donovan smile.

"Now he can say 'we' about Morna and himself—about the Rosses as well as the Hendersons," Hope went on earnestly. "He's begun to see how wonderful it is to have a real sister. I told him I'd always wished I had had a sister—I'm an only child. And I tried to show him that it won't make any difference to the Hendersons —that he's really just as much a son to them even though he is Morna's brother. But now he won't have to pretend any more. And we'll all like him better, won't we?"

"Sure we will," Stevie said, but she smiled at Al so he wouldn't have anything to worry about.

Butch said, "There's your father, Stevie—" And Stevie turned to see Daddy and Mother just coming in.

"Hey, did you catch the crooks?" Lyle called. Dad smiled and hugged Lyle while Mother hugged Stevie, and then Stevie introduced them both to Morna.

"We didn't have to," Dad answered Lyle. "They had been caught by some alert officers who never even knew they were kidnapers."

The boys had stood up and now they found chairs for Stevie's parents. Al asked them if they'd like some ice cream, and Mother said they'd love some.

"I figured they'd be caught," Lyle told Dad. He said

to Stevie, "That's why I left Sport with them. See, I knew if those crooks were stopped for any reason—like for the speeding they were doing when they left us—and the police saw Sport in the car, they'd be arrested for transporting a walking catfish without a permit. So they were, huh, Dad?" he added complacently.

"They were," Dad confirmed solemnly. "For speeding and for possessing and transporting a *Clarias* catfish without a permit. Also for sideswiping Bill's truck, which they were seen to do from a distance, and for leaving the scene of an accident *and* for kidnaping. By the way, Lieutenant Ellis says you can have Sport back any time now. He'll be glad to see the last of him."

"Let's go by for him on the way home," Lyle said. "I'll give old Sport a certificate of commendation myself if Lieutenant Ellis doesn't appreciate his help in catching criminals."

Tinky said to Morna, "So your aunt and uncle won't have any more trouble with James and the others for a while. They'll be in jail."

"I'm glad," Morna said. "And Hughie can be heir to Rossholm and still be the Hendersons' son. I'm glad about that too. Ian's a real fine Scottish name."

Stevie told Mother, "Morna's going to stay with us till she goes back to her aunt's and uncle's, O.K.?"

"Of course," Mother said.

When they were all leaving the Apothecary's for the Square to hear the Barbershop Quartet, Bill said, "Funny

how everything's still going on at the Square, just as if none of the excitement had ever happened! Things haven't changed a bit."

But Stevie knew things had changed. For some of them. For Morna and Ian, at least. And for herself. She didn't feel the same inside about Ian. She felt kinder, and softer, and—well, not mean any more.

And then Hope caught her arm and made her linger a little bit behind the others to tell her, "Stevie—Ian asked me to go with him next Friday to My Brother's Top Drawer! To hear him sing the song he wrote about me!" She sounded 'way up on cloud nine, and her gray eyes were big and shining.

"Great!" Stevie said, and she was proud of herself

for not feeling the least bit envious, only glad for Hope. Then things had changed for Hope too.

"And," Hope confided shyly, "he said 'we'll go.' *We*."

"Hey," Stevie warned, "don't let him think you belong to him!"

"Oh," Hope said, "do you think he ever could?"